Author's Note

This book is a work of fiction. Although the photograph by Steve McCurry of the Afghan refugee commonly referred to as *Afghan Girl* that appeared most famously on the cover of *National Geographic* served as inspiration for certain aspects of this novel, in no way are the characters of Ethan and Setara depicted in these pages meant to represent McCurry or his subject, Sharbat Gula. All the characters and events in the novel are entirely the products of my imagination, and any resemblance to actual persons, living or dead, or actual events is coincidental.

For my mother
Evelyn Mason Newberry (1933–2018)
who shared my love of books
and for my father
Thomas Lee Newberry (1933–2018)
who told me I could do anything I set my mind to

You just missed it.

TIDAL FLATS

"Tidal Flats is the inherently compelling, deftly crafted, and remarkably original story of a marriage this is all the more impressive when considering that it is author Cynthia Newberry Martin's debut as a novelist."

—Midwest Book Review

"At around the halfway mark of *Tidal Flats,* once I got past wanting to throw it across the Marta train and wring one of the character's necks, I remember thinking, 'I just want all books to be like this.' Kudos to Cynthia Newberry Martin. You created something raw, real, and beautiful, a lovely piece of art that was near impossible for me to put down. Thank you!"

—Kim Ware, singer, songwriter, musician of The Good Graces

"Thoughtful and nuanced, Cynthia Newberry Martin's masterful sentences build a gripping narrative about how the best of intentions can fracture a marriage. *Tidal Flats* reminds readers that love is a verb, a decision, a choice one decides to make each day. Martin explores the conflicting obligations individuals agree to in devotion to partners, professions, and communities, local and abroad. Cass and Ethan's journey reflects the strength we all might find in compromise, in choosing to be open to loss. It's a remarkable story about how promises can shatter and reshape the life one thinks they should live."

—Donald Quist, author of *Harbors*

"In novels or dramas about fraught romantic relationships, the narrative often feels bent toward disintegration, with the possibility—and sometimes the inevitability—of separation looming over every scene. What distinguishes Cynthia Newberry Martin's debut novel, *Tidal Flats,* is how deeply it immerses us in one character's process of figuring out what might be lost or gained by staying in a seriously challenged relationship, or by moving on from it. The outcome of her process never feels certain nor inevitable, and the result is a captivating and illuminating read."

—Beth Castrodale, Small Press Picks

"I was captivated by the stunning, graceful quality of the prose as well as by the wisdom in her descriptions of both personal and interpersonal dynamics. The tension and pacing of the story kept me intrigued, and I appreciated her economy of language as the story unfolded. *Tidal Flats* is a refreshing read in that it doesn't gloss over or minimize issues contemporary couples face. I recommend it to anyone who wants to read an excellent novel about love, and marriage, with a psychological bent."

—Catherine McCall, author of *Never Tell*

"Cynthia Newberry Martin has created a cast of familiar yet unforgettable characters. With great skill, she plops us into the marriage of Cass and Ethan, which is founded in love and an agreement they name *Tidal Flats*. But the agreement unravels as Ethan begins to grow and change. Unable to let go of long-held beliefs based on a childhood trauma, Cass is stuck and unable to give her husband what he needs. Until a number of surprises turns her life upside down and forces her onto a journey of self-discovery, which makes for such a compelling read, I didn't want it to end."

—Darrelyn Saloom, author of *My Call to the Ring*

"This debut novel explores what happens when two people start their marriage with an agreement, a three-year contract that they hope will give them each what they need for the rest of their lives together. The idea intrigued me—the pact made by two very different people, Cass and Ethan, is born of great love but also a desire to accommodate their conflicting desires and fears. Even if they remain in love, can their agreement survive three years of absences, long distance and be the seed for a lasting marriage? It's a risky proposition, but then marriage itself is a risky proposition. Martin tells the story of these two people with a wonderful mix of fearlessness and compassion and brings us to a conclusion that is satisfying even as it raises questions about what we can control and what we can't."

—Elizabeth Marro, author of *Casualties*

Praise for *Tidal Flats*

Gold Medal in Literary Fiction at the 2020 Independent
Publisher Book Awards
14th Annual National Indie Excellence Award for Fiction

"With deep insight and unending sensitivity, Cynthia Newberry Martin shows us to ourselves: our penchant for choosing lives that will crack us open, our resilience when our deepest fears come true. In scenes both vivid and emotionally complex, *Tidal Flats* excavates the interior of a long-term marriage, how it demands the impossible, offers the unimaginable. This book is a stunning, heart-expanding debut."

—Pam Houston, author of *Deep Creek: Finding Hope in the High Country*

"Cynthia Newberry Martin's *Tidal Flats* is written out of the rough wisdom that knows that love is a peculiar, dynamic force, and all we can do against it is to be alert and open and awake. This is a story of making and unmaking and making again, with no neat resolutions or pat answers. It's a beautiful book."

—Paul Lisicky, author of *Later* and *The Narrow Door*

"Cynthia Newberry Martin is a tremendous writer, with a Woolfian talent for taking the full measure of small moments. Her work is both subtle and revelatory, and I've been waiting a long time for this book."

—Rebecca Makkai, author of *The Great Believers*

"For once, a novel of big ideas that is also filled with bold and uncommon events. In *Tidal Flats*, Cynthia Newberry Martin, a storyteller at the top of her game, creates a universe of betrayal, compassion, and regret in which two people's love for each other is surpassed only by their loyalty to their convictions."

—Jacquelyn Mitchard, author of *The Deep End of the Ocean*

"I admire Martin's capacity to render her characters with the dignity of complexity. And I double-admire that she takes that same care with her settings, turning Place into a player that has its own 'human' heart. The novel swirls with light and love."

—Joshua Mohr, author of *Sirens* and *Damascus*

"Exquisite! A gorgeously observed account of one woman's life, lived in our era of global reach, of international obligations, of domestic worries and domestic triumphs too. Cynthia Newberry Martin has found the perfect story through which to share her rare wisdom. Brava!"

—Robin Black, author of *Life Drawing*

"I'm absolutely smitten with the entire cast of unforgettable characters, from Cass to Ethan to Singer to the marvelous Howell House women. Via this rich story of love, marriage, choices, place, longing, and desire, Cynthia Newberry Martin beautifully reveals the vulnerabilities in all of us. This novel deserves big love in the world."

—Kristin Bair O'Keeffe, author of *Agatha Arch Is Afraid of Everything*

"Finally, a beautiful and surprising love story about a married couple! Cass and Ethan want what we all want: choices, the comfort of home and family. And freedom. They make plans and a pact, oblivious to the sucker punch to come. *Tidal Flats* is an important, honest debut novel that deals with the consequences of love, war, and forgiveness. The ending will take your breath away."

—Margaret McMullan, author of *Where the Angels Lived*

TIDAL FLATS

A NOVEL

by

CYNTHIA NEWBERRY MARTIN

bonhomie press

CORAL GABLES

Cover Design: Morgane Leoni
Cover Photo: © Wirestock / Adobe Stock
Art Direction: Morgane Leoni

Grateful acknowledgement is made to Coleman Barks for permission to reprint excerpts from *The Essential Rumi*.

For permission requests, please contact the publisher at:
Mango Publishing Group
2850 S Douglas Road, 4th Floor
Coral Gables, FL 33134 USA
info@mango.bz

For special orders, quantity sales, course adoptions and corporate sales, please email the publisher at sales@mango.bz. For trade and wholesale sales, please contact Ingram Publisher Services at customer.service@ingramcontent.com or +1.800.509.4887.

Tidal Flats: A Novel

Library of Congress Cataloging-in-Publication number: 2022935588
ISBN: (print) 978-1-64250-981-6, (ebook) 978-1-64250-982-3
BISAC category code FIC045010, FICTION / Family Life / Marriage & Divorce

Printed in the United States of America

Listen to the story told by the reed,
of being separated.

"Since I was cut from the reedbed,
I have made this crying sound.

Anyone apart from someone he loves
understands what I say.

Anyone pulled from a source
longs to go back."

—Rumi

The darkness that night contained three things: a wife in Atlanta, a husband in Afghanistan, and an agreement that was to hold them together forever. In Atlanta, after Cass turned off her lamp, she paused. The darkness was always there, always waiting for the light to go out. When the hand of the alarm clock she and Ethan had bought together ticked to the next second, she lay down and pulled the thin spring covers over her shoulders all the way up to her neck. Underneath the darkness was where she slept; it was where we all slept. A phone ringing in the middle of the night didn't so much break the darkness as become the sound of it.

The Agreement

When Cass and Ethan had been going out a year, they rented a friend's cottage in the west end of Provincetown, and the June weather cooperated—a crisp warm during the day and cool at night—until the last day when they were socked in with fog and rain. The windows had been open but now were stuck. Being her mother's child, Cass leaned her forehead on the pane, allowing glass to stand in the way of what she wanted. But after a while, she straightened. Every problem, her father had always said, was just a problem to solve. She found tools in a toolbox and pried the bayside windows open. Then she closed her eyes, drinking in the salt spray and listening to the comforting sound of the foghorn.

Ethan came up and reached behind her, crossing easily into her territory, bending for her black sweatshirt that had fallen to the floor and returning it to her.

"Let's go out there," he said. "In it."

Wearing old baseball caps and slickers, they grabbed water bottles and headed farther west. Usually, they walked past the breakwater on a mission for the beach, but this day they had no mission and veered left to take a closer look at the magical, man-made rock pathway that struck out across the water, splitting it into harbor and marsh and leading to the fingertips of the fist of the very, very end of Cape Cod.

Ethan stepped through the opening in the fence. "C'mon," he said, turning toward her.

It was just past high tide, and the water was full and rough, uncontained, splashing against the boulders. Out here, unprotected, the wind was stronger, throwing the rain around. One bird—a black-headed, orange-beaked tern—bumped up and down with the gusts, holding steady but making no progress.

At the start, the rocks were close together and stepping from one to another was easy, but they were rain-soaked and slippery, and Cass didn't risk lifting her gaze from the next spot her foot would go. Then the gaps increased. One small misstep and her leg would be wedged between these rocks that were alike and different—sharp and uneven and every shade of gray with streaks of pink and yellow and green. She yelled ahead, asking Ethan if it was granite.

He stopped. "Did you say something?"

She repeated her question, staring at him standing there on top of a giant boulder in the middle of rushing water.

He nodded. "Brought over from Quincy in the early 1900s I think."

"Ethan."

He turned toward her again.

"It's like Stone Mountain. It's like...I don't know, but I think it means something."

He held his arms out to the side and tilted his head. "Granite's our rock?"

"Well, we're official now," she said, grinning. "We have a rock."

The night Cass met Ethan, he'd told her he felt more himself in Afghanistan than anywhere else. Three months later, at Stone Mountain on a humid day in August, she'd told him she wanted a husband who came home at night and that she didn't think she wanted children. They had continued the climb in silence; she assumed they were done. But they hadn't gone far when, standing on the mountain granite, he'd pulled her to him and told her that things had changed. Now he felt more himself with her than anywhere in the world.

The wind fell silent, and Cass could hear the foghorn. The breakwater would land them between two opposing lighthouses—one flashing a green light and the other, red. She paused, unsure at first which one was sounding, but both were, as if talking to each other. Then the wind picked up again, and she couldn't hear either one, which was disconcerting. No one else was crazy enough to be out.

Some boulders tended to the horizontal, others to the vertical; some spread out long and lean; others topped out fat and jagged; some lay smooth side up, others corner up—but all as if some massive hand had dropped them from the sky and left them however they fell. On the surface of some, pools of water collected; on others, broken bits of seashells. And there were the things that had washed up—a rainbow Hula-Hoop, one red flip-flop, a stalk of bamboo.

Something clattered onto a rock in front of her. A seagull swooped down and picked up a mollusk and dropped it again. Three times, as she stood there transfixed. The last drop cracked the shell.

The gaps between rocks became wider still. In some places, she couldn't step but had to jump. In one spot, she had to use her hands and knees to make it to the next rock. Ahead, Ethan had stopped. She came up behind him, and he reached back for her hand.

In front of them, two long, narrow boulders, side by side.

She sat down—she was already soaked—facing the direction from which they had come. Ethan sat behind her, his back against hers, facing the steps they had yet to take. The tide was on its way out, the water singing through the rocks beneath them. That tern, which had seemed stationary, joined them now, wings outstretched.

"So," he said.

"I know," she said.

He leaned against her; she leaned back with equal force. And then there was no force, just the lean—just the two of them leaning on each other.

"It's a country of contrasts and divisions," Ethan said. "Compartments."

Lost in the world around her, she had no idea what he was talking about.

"Nangarhar province is green, but a lot of the country is dry and mountainous. They build walls everywhere. People will create a village around a river so they have access to the water they need to survive, only to be wiped out by that same river during the spring thaw and floods."

"I don't want to go to Afghanistan," she said. "Even with you."

"I just thought if you saw it—"

"I'd understand why my father had to die there."

"You'd understand why I love it."

She took a sip of water, felt how easily she swallowed it, thought how easily Afghanistan would swallow her. She'd disappear.

"Three years," he said. "That's all I'm asking."

"We should just wait then, until you're done."

"I want to belong to you now," he said. "I want us to shape our lives together. I don't want to end up ten years from now with nothing but Afghanistan."

The rock beneath her was rough despite its smooth appearance. Running her fingers back and forth, she asked, "What are you looking for when you take your photos?"

"Too many things, it sometimes seems. Differing elements coming together in one moment, complications, surprising myself, color. Definitely color."

"The words *husband* and *wife*," she said. "Those words change things."

"They're just words," he said.

"They're possessive."

"But I want *you* to possess *me*," he said. "Right this minute." He rubbed his head back against hers at the same time that he reached his hands behind him and grabbed her hips. "What if I hadn't found you?"

"What if I hadn't found you?" she said.

"*Husband* and *wife* aren't possessive words," he said. "They're belonging words. They mean we each have a place in the world where we belong."

She closed her eyes. The possibility of belonging was at the same time too much and still not enough. She opened her eyes and saw houses, the shoreline, the monument and the library guarding the town. "What do you see your way?" she asked.

"A lighthouse, the marsh, uninhabited land."

His bones to her bones. She'd been alone all her life it sometimes seemed. She knew alone; she could control it. This new country, shining off in the distance, scared her even as it drew her toward it.

"How about this," he said. "For three years, I'll keep going back and forth to Afghanistan. And you'll work on imagining our family. After three years, no more Afghanistan. I'll limit travel to one night, maybe two. And if you don't change your mind about a baby, then we won't have any. I get what I want first, but you get what you want forever."

An agreement. She breathed out. The agreement felt safe. It made a space for each of them. She turned to face him—this man who understood her as no one ever had. Even she hadn't thought of planning for love.

"It may always be just the two of us," he said, "but it *will be* the two of us."

And this was more than she could resist.

She leaned over and kissed him. He kissed the top of her head.

"We need a name," she said.

"A name?"

"For the agreement. To make it real."

"It's already real," he said.

But she knew the power of words. "We're out here in the middle of this space that is sometimes water and sometimes sand. Is there a name for out here?"

"Tidal flats," he said and looked at her.

"The Tidal Flats Agreement," she said.

And he held out his little finger, which she hooked with hers. Then he pulled her to him and kissed her and asked her to spend the rest of her life with him. They helped each other stand and continued on. Up ahead she was surprised to see that the rocks veered quite dramatically to the left. When they'd started out, it had looked like a straight shot.

1

To Cass, he was just Ethan, the man she'd been married to for almost three years, the man who curled into a ball as he slept and who liked to read *People* magazine, but to the rest of the world, he was the photojournalist behind *The Afghan Woman* and the famous *Portraits of Afghanistan*. He was the "Photographer with the Soul of a Nation."

With no direct flight from Kabul, he came home by way of Dubai, the nonstop due in at 6:06 a.m. Add to that delays, customs, baggage claim. She didn't just pull up to the curb; she'd made it a ritual to park and go inside, to sit in the atrium drinking coffee while she waited for his text, then to stand behind the roped-off area that assured arriving passengers of enough space to exit, her eyes locked on the airport escalator on the other side of the empty corridor watching for his curly black hair. Watching his tired eyes find hers. His ears like wings, no smile—that was Ethan. Which made her smile.

Instead of navigating around the rope, he came straight to her and dropped a bag from each hand, wrapping his arms and body around her, the rope between them nothing after sixty-three days—the longest they'd ever been apart. Only then, when she could smell the tangy shaving cream he'd used in the airplane bathroom, did she allow herself to feel every drop of missing him, that wave knocking her under at the same time that it began to recede.

Sometimes, even before their apartment door shut all the way, they began to shed their clothes, leaving a trail to the shower. Their first meal—eggs and bacon, toast with jam—eaten standing in the light-filled kitchen, each of them by that point too hungry to wait.

Day two just the opposite, unfurling in slow motion. For the sake of time zones, they would plan to rise at a normal time but could never do it. When eventually they did, she would sit on the counter while he made coffee, happy he didn't like the way she made it so she could watch him roam the kitchen where he seemed more like something exotic than something that belonged. They would stay in their pajamas, watch movies, do his laundry. Day three would take the shape of a day, but one with a deckle edge. Computers on laps opened as an afterthought, some part of him touching some part of her. But by day four, neither could resist the siren call of the real world.

On this day four, as they lay in bed, jackhammers from the construction site across the street revved up. Ethan jumped. She reached for him, but he was already standing, and her arms landed in the warm indentation where he no longer was. He picked up a pillow from the floor and threw it at her, something the first one to leave the bed often did, their way of saying they didn't want to leave the other behind. She turned to watch him cross the room, her eyes fixing on the boomerang-shaped scar that dipped below his waist until he disappeared into the bathroom.

With one kick, she extricated her feet from the sheets and rolled out of bed to their wall of windows. Sunlight peeking from behind the buildings in downtown Atlanta. Between here and there, traffic on the connector. The green on the trees, sparse but already there, now at the beginning of March. It would only be a matter of months before everything fell into place—Ethan home for good and Cass in charge at Howell. Planning, that's all life took. A little planning.

She could hear the shower, could feel the humidity rising. Ethan almost never shut doors. He said he didn't want anything between them. But there were often continents between them. And that endless gray ocean.

But soon there wouldn't be. She stretched, feeling the world expanding around her. The windows misted over. She drew a heart with her finger and felt like a teenager. They were about to enter a new phase, one where *alone* would finally be wiped off the map. The shower stopped, and she looked over her shoulder. When she turned back to the window, the heart was already gone.

Ethan emerged with a towel around his waist. She tapped the ottoman away and stepped backward into the easy chair, sitting with her knees to her chest. Boxers, button-down, jeans. Soon he'd head to his studio, but he'd be home later this same day—like a normal husband.

"Sorry about the timing of this Boston trip," he said, glancing over while threading his belt through the loops. "I'm not ready to leave you yet."

"Sometimes you are?"

He tilted his head in her direction as he sat on the end of the bed. Brown socks, city boots.

"Supper request?" she said.

He stood and scooped his wallet from the oblong wooden bowl on top of the dresser, then he leaned over her, his hands on the arms of the chair.

Normally, she didn't enjoy being trapped.

"Why don't you come with me?" he said.

"To Boston?"

"Think about it." And he tweaked her nose as if he were about to claim he'd stolen it by showing her his thumb. "You know I don't care about dinner."

"Maybe I'll just grab something from the market."

He left the room, and she hopped up, getting to the front door in time to hold it open, in time for the kiss that only had to last eight hours.

Before he disappeared down their third-floor hallway, he turned and said, "Tidal Flats, babe."

She smiled, eased the door closed, and leaned back against

it. Sunlight poured through their French doors, filling the room. The morning in full force. After three days of Ethan, she missed the Fates.

$$\circ \; O \; \circ$$

In the bathroom, she picked up her fat-toothed comb and parted her straight, blonde hair in the middle. At the end of December, right after Ethan left, she'd had it cut shoulder-length, but now the ends fell down her back again.

She adjusted her light gray towel on the bar and then took Ethan's dark gray one off, refolded it, and hung it back, all the while wondering if he were done, or if he would try to squeeze one last trip into the nine weeks that stretched like a suspension bridge across a deep and wide gully, their anniversary on the other side.

Bathroom light off, covers up on her side of the bed, and on his. Married. Before Ethan, she hadn't even held this picture in her head; she wouldn't have known how to.

She stepped out of the apartment, closed the door, and headed toward the elevator. He always told her as soon as he knew he was going back. Sometimes a trip would be planned weeks in advance, and sometimes he'd be leaving that night. She was used to not knowing *when*. What was different this time was not knowing *if*.

2

Howell House could accommodate three residents, and the staff had referred to these three women as the Fates for as long as Cass had worked there. No one knew who'd first given them the name or how it had been intended, but Cass took it as a sign.

On her way over, she avoided the sidewalk cracks as if she were trying to make sure she stepped on solid ground. *Look up*—May was always telling her to look up—and there were the lacy pink and white flowers of the dogwood trees. Columbus was where she'd first seen them—the four strong petals, flawed around the edges, surrounding the heart center.

At the coffee shop, her usual medium latte with coconut milk. Back on the sidewalk, as her steps quickened, her worn canvas messenger bag rubbed against her thigh. Inside the bag, her slim laptop and a copy of *The Heart Is a Lonely Hunter*, the first book she'd read to May almost four years ago. Now May wanted to read the book again. At the intersection, Cass stopped and took a sip of coffee.

"Is he home?" Vee asked, out of breath.

"Where'd you come from?"

"I saw you from the bus." Vee was thirty-two, three years older than Cass, and tall, with shiny, black hair that looked as if she'd taken the scissors to it herself, in the dark.

"Is that glitter in your hair?" Cass asked.

"You like it?"

"I do, actually."

"How is he?"

"Wonderful."

"Maybe if Dillon left for two months, he'd be wonderful when he got back."

"Ha," Cass said, leaning forward to push the button. According to Vee, Dillon was an alcoholic and Heathcliff-ish. Cass had never met him. Ethan hung out with her and Vee every once in a while, but she and Vee were friends, not the four of them.

"Those buttons don't do anything," Vee said. "They're there to make you think you have control."

Cass stared at the light, willing it to change. "He might be home for good."

"I don't care what the two of you agreed to," Vee said, her hand waving in the air as if it wanted to fly away, and her tattoo—a tiny bird in flight toward her wrist—sneaking out of her sleeve. "Everybody in the world wants *The Afghan Woman* guy to keep going to Afghanistan."

Cars passed in a blur. "I thought you were on *my* side."

"You know I am."

"He brought up the agreement himself this morning."

"And I woke up thinking about it," Vee said. "But I mean, do you want to be that person, the woman who stopped him from going back?"

Cass stepped away from the curb and looked at Vee. "*I'm* not stopping him. He wants *more* than just Afghanistan. The agreement was *his* idea."

"Right," Vee said, but she might as well have rolled her eyes.

The wind gusted. Cass turned her head to the sky.

"Perfect day to knock hang gliding off the list," Vee said.

Vee's lists. One with things she wanted to learn how to do and the other with things she was afraid to do, which made her want to do them. Mostly, she and Vee were two of a kind, but instead of going after the things she was afraid of, Cass avoided them.

"Aren't you going the wrong way for the library?" Cass said.

"Health center. Out of birth control pills. What did he bring you this time?"

"This handmade journal the size of my palm. With a papery light green cover and this delicate green thread that wraps around it."

"I just love the way he brings you things."

The light changed, and they started across Howell Mill, each knocking into the other between the white lines.

"Singer sends his regards," Vee said. Singer was the artist bartender where she and Vee hung out—where Vee went almost every day after work. Cass joined her when Ethan was gone.

"Back at him," Cass said, thinking of his red hair and warm smile. Singer was a bright light at the end of a long day—and he was *always* here.

As they separated on the other side of the street, Vee waved over her head.

But Cass felt as if she'd forgotten something, and it took her a few seconds to land on Vee's words about Ethan's famous *TIME* cover. When she did, she told herself *not now*, steering her thoughts back to reading to May, who'd made it to ninety-three but who, according to her doctor, wouldn't live much longer. She'd told Cass, "It's my heart. I used it up. Isn't that grand? I didn't waste any of it."

At the entrance to the deserted parking lot that had once been Hattie Howell's front yard, Cass tripped over a tree root but recovered without falling. Maybe the staff should park out here. Energy was what this place needed. And music. Open windows. But at the moment, all the windows were painted shut.

3

At Howell's front door, Cass used her key. Hattie Howell hadn't had any children, and when she died at ninety-six, her will created a foundation to run a home for older women. She wanted other people to have the benefit of aging as she had—in a real home. Plus, she wanted them to have something she hadn't had—the benefit of living with others. In the foyer, a sofa sat against the back wall and in front of it, a coffee table with a bowl of lemons—real. That had been Cass's first suggestion. Real lemons made it an entirely different place.

"It's me," she yelled.

"Morning," Ella yelled from the back of the house.

Off the foyer to the right was Bev's glass office—regal Bev with milky smooth Black skin. Cass unlocked the door. She didn't have an office and would usually sit in the breakfast room or the kitchen to make notes or file reports. She had more contact with the Fates, whereas Bev managed the staff, the finances, the regulations. Cass was the Fate liaison; Bev, the board liaison.

But when Bev was not here, like this week, with Ella's help, Cass did it all. She dropped her stuff on the desk. And in six more months, Bev would retire, and Cass would do it all *all the time.*

As she started for the kitchen, the phone rang.

"I knew you'd be there early," Bev said. "Ethan back okay?"

"Yep, all good," Cass said, sitting down.

"So," Bev said, her voice different, flat, "I'm sorry to have to talk to you about this over the phone and right when Ethan's back."

Cass heard her take a breath. "Bev?"

"I need you to take over now instead of at the end of the year. The foundation has approved."

"What? *Why?*" Cass couldn't make sense of it.

"I've gotten some bad news." She paused. "Bone cancer."

"Oh my God, Bev," Cass stood. "I'm so sorry."

"But I'm happy for you. This is what you've been waiting for and working toward. You deserve it."

"But are you going to be okay? And your retirement."

"The doctors think I have a decent chance. I'll be okay. Hopefully." Then in her typical Bev way, she was all business. "Letters will go out to the families tomorrow, so tell the Fates and Ella and Fanny the day after. You're a natural, you know. You have been since...well, I won't say since you walked in the door, but since your first conversation with May. I know that. The foundation knows that. Follow your instincts."

That first day, two and a half years ago, the front porch had been covered in brilliant burgundy leaves. Cass had seen a flyer at Vee's library. That's what she used to do when she wasn't working for the boring accountant—hang out at the library, which Ethan, always on the lookout for danger, complained was too close to the jail. But Cass loved being around books, and she loved to read, always had. She loved words.

The bright orange flyer on the library bulletin board announced that Howell House, just around the corner, needed people to read to the older women who could no longer see, and it wasn't so much that something clicked into place as that Cass felt some soft thing inside her. When she'd arrived, Bev suggested she start by talking to May, who had Cass's grandmother's white hair. And although Cass had not signed on for talking, she felt the soft thing again. As the weeks then years went by, Cass became like that perfume that smells different on each person—able to figure out what each Fate needed and help her get it. Except for May. All this time and Cass had yet to figure out how she could help May.

In January, Bev had pulled her aside and told her she'd be retiring at the end of the year and that she, and the board, wanted Cass to take over when she did—something Cass had already been dreaming of. But to have it happen like this was not part of the plan, and she felt terrible for Bev, who'd been looking forward to traveling with her husband and to visiting grandchildren. Now there would be hospitals, and someone would need to help *her*.

"If there's anything I can do, Bev, just let me know."

"You're doing it," she said.

Cass sat down. Now this was her office. Three of the walls were floor-to-ceiling windows—out the front, the gravel parking area; out the side, a line of pyramid cedars; out the back, a deck. And everywhere, those old oak trees. But it was the fourth wall, the original brick exterior of the house that with the addition of this room had become an interior wall, which made what had just happened seem real. Cass stood and ran her hands over its rough surface.

$$\circ \,^\circ \circ$$

In the kitchen, Fanny, their cook, looked up from the counter where she was squeezing lemons into a pitcher and nodded at Cass, who pushed open the swinging door into the adjacent breakfast room, where the Fates were still at the table.

"How is everybody?" Cass said, gazing at the Black and white faces, at Atta's slicked-back charcoal gray hair that she kept in a long braid, and at Lois's not blonde but yellow hair.

"How are *you*, Mary Cassatt Miller?" Atta said, as she continued cutting an article out of the newspaper, her plate pushed away as if she were through but she never was.

"Lois, welcome," Cass said, sitting in May's empty chair. "Sorry to miss your arrival." Lois had taken Ruth Ann's room. Ruth Ann who could never remember to put her teeth in. A couple of weeks ago, she had wandered, and if they wandered, they had to go.

Lois half-smiled, half-grimaced, her lipstick every bit as red as Atta's—at breakfast—as she picked up a measuring cup and poured the rest of the cream into her coffee. "Is that really your middle name?" she asked.

Cass nodded. "Painting was my mother's dream. Are you settled in?"

"They wouldn't let me bring all my stuff."

"Who?" Cass asked.

"It's all just clutter, the kids said."

"Is there something in particular you miss?"

Lois peered at her through her old lady, mother-of-pearl frames. "I keep thinking about my red heels. They have this diagonal strap across the top. Richard bought them for me in Italy. Our twenty-fifth wedding anniversary. I haven't worn them in twenty years."

"Let me see what I can do." Cass turned to Ella. "May?"

"Not feeling well this morning."

"Again," Atta said.

Ella, who worked 7 a.m. to 7 p.m., raised her eyebrows and held onto her coffee. Her mother was Spanish, and Ella had inherited that Spanish flair. She was young and still lived at home and did not yet have a mind of her own. But she was smart and dependable and loved the Fates almost as much as Cass. "It started Saturday," she said. "Fanny's been taking her a tray."

Cass pushed the scissors back from the edge of the table as Atta reached for the biscuit on her plate and added a giant spoonful of strawberry jam.

"So," Ella said, her dark eyes wide, "does absence make the heart grow fonder?"

"More importantly," Atta said, "How was the sex?"

"Atta," Ella said. "Boundaries."

"I'm against them," Atta said. "I wonder how many years it's been since I had sex. That could be another one of your improvements, Cass, another service offered by Howell." And she popped the loaded biscuit into her mouth.

Cass and Ella laughed. Fanny was laughing in the kitchen. "Request noted," Cass said. "Are the two of you sharing lipstick?"

"It wouldn't hurt you to put on some, too," Atta said, holding a napkin in front of her mouth so she could continue chewing and talk.

"You don't give up, do you, Atta?"

"I do not."

Some women had to learn to be more self-sufficient, like Ruth Ann who had asked permission for everything, and others, due to the restrictions of age, had to make peace with being less, like Atta. Wherever they were in the process, Cass wanted them to have things to look forward to. She wanted Howell to be about living.

"Who's doing something fun today?"

"I'm walking in Piedmont Park," Atta said. "The van leaves at 9:30 if anybody else wants to go." She glanced over at Lois. Now that Ruth Ann was gone, Atta was their youngest at eighty-three.

"I do," Lois said.

Fanny, in her sun yellow carpenter's apron, stepped into the breakfast room to say she'd fixed a couple of bags of old bread for the ducks.

"I'm going to exercise," Atta said.

"I'll take a bag," Lois said. And then to Atta, "In case I can't keep up with you."

The duck pond at Piedmont Park was where Ethan had first told Cass he loved her. While he was taking photos, she'd been watching the squawking ducks flap their wings. He'd come up behind her, lifted her long hair off her neck, and whispered into her ear. She leaned back against him, needing his warmth. The last person to tell her he loved her had been her father. Cass turned and looked into Ethan's dark eyes. She loved him too and told him. Then she turned away again, pulling his arms around her and holding on to them, searching out beyond the pond as far as she could see and trying to see farther, wondering how long it would be before he was gone too.

4

Cass's father had been a lieutenant general hoping for a fourth star. Ten years ago, just after he died, she'd flown to MacDill Air Force Base in Tampa, where he'd been stationed before he deployed. She couldn't find his book of Rumi's poems anywhere. A month later, when the box of his things arrived from Afghanistan, there it was.

When she'd left the apartment this morning, everything was the same; now she was returning home in charge of Howell. Once in the door, she went straight to her desk for her father's leather-bound copy of Rumi. The spine was broken, the pages torn and discolored, but in a book of 225 pages, only five passages were marked, each by two lines, one in the white space to the side of the passage and one under a word in the passage. Cass knew all five by heart. When she was a child, her father had read to her, not from children's books but from Rumi. Since her father died, she'd read the book a crazy number of times. And every time, only those ten ruler-straight lines. When she came across an underlined word, she placed her finger on it. *Emptiness, love, wings, darkness, fire*—this was the order the words appeared in the passages in the book, but often she rearranged them, trying to turn them into a message.

She placed Rumi back on top of the stack of books on her smoky white desk, the only piece of furniture that had made the journey from house number fourteen in Columbus to her college dorm suite in downtown Atlanta. In her Virginia Highlands apartment, the only place the desk had fit was next to her bed, saving her the cost of a separate night table. Now next to her bed was the only place her desk felt right—fueling her dreams and standing guard.

In the den, she stretched out on the sofa not looking toward the French doors that opened onto the world of the city where, with all the metal and glass, everything seemed alive—quick, sharp, shiny—but looking toward the motionless front door. At the scratching sound of a key in the lock, she looked up, and there was Ethan—and as if she were a match he'd struck, a spark ran through her body, from her eyes through her heart to her toes. The shock and pleasure of it. His coming home and her being here. Marriage.

Before she could get up, he bent to kiss her, sliding his hand down her arm until his fingers slipped between her fingers—making her want to reverse time so she could watch to see how their fingers knew which way to go.

As he straightened, he pulled a bottle of champagne out of a brown paper bag. "Congratulations to the new director," he said.

She grinned and pulled him down for another kiss. "Thank you," she said. "Although it's terrible about Bev."

"She's tough. I bet she comes through even stronger."

He dropped his computer and camera cases on the wheelbarrow bench—made from an Afghan wheelbarrow with one side cut off and a blue cushion added. With a sigh, he collapsed on the sofa that backed up to hers. They had two identical sofas, one facing the fireplace and the other facing the TV.

"How was your day?" she asked, words she loved saying. She reached over the low backs of the sofas and rubbed his shoulder through the black cashmere sweater she'd given him before they were married.

"I got the photos off to Boston. Only a month late. And listen to this. I'm just going to use one room, square, with one glass door. Nineteen photos. All the same size. All hung at the same height. Black frames, of course. Five photos on each wall—except the wall with the door." He sat up on his elbows as if he wanted to make sure she was listening. "The photos—of the war, the people, the land—no beginning or end."

"I love it," she said, climbing, as she often did, onto the tops of the sofas, leaving one leg on her side and wedging the other one in beside Ethan, who dropped his head back to the sofa arm. "I do want to go with you."

"That's my girl," he said. "I'll see about getting you a ticket." He picked up her foot and placed it on his chest. Then he peeled off her sock and held onto her bare foot.

○ ○ ○

In their galley kitchen, Ethan stood there, his hands in his pockets, while on their small island she assembled the mustard, pimentos, softened cream cheese, and bowl of grated cheddar. He loved it when she made her grandmother's pimento cheese.

"How's the new Fate?" he asked, leaning toward her.

"Lois. She's eighty-six. She has children and grandchildren and great-grandchildren."

"I wonder what being eighty-six feels like—having your life behind you."

Cass stopped stirring, looked at Ethan. "She's not dead."

"But babe, scientifically speaking..."

"E, these years count as much as the others. I refuse to accept that the Fates are just waiting to die." She leaned against the counter. "But they're fifty years older than we are," she said. "Fifty. That seems impossible. Lois's kids wouldn't let her bring everything she wanted to."

He pulled out their single kitchen stool and sat, watching her.

"There's this pair of red heels," she said, stirring again.

"Heels?"

"Yes, heels. The man who once loved her like you love me gave them to her. He's dead, and now she doesn't even have the shoes."

"If you get them for her, then one day, fifty years from now, maybe someone will retrieve something I gave you, that our children make you give away."

"How do you do that—turn a conversation so completely?"

$$\circ \,^\circ \circ$$

Two plates, two glasses, two of everything. Which made her think of Noah and wonder what was coming.

"While you were in the shower," he said, "I checked about getting you a ticket to Boston. Not many options since I'm going up one day and coming back the next. Almost a thousand dollars."

"Because you leave in eleven days. But who's counting?"

He tilted his head and took another bite of Chicken Parmesan. They were eating on the table that had been in her apartment. Two candles.

"That's an absurd amount of money," she said, twirling her wine glass. "And Boston's just one night." One night was not a problem. One night was a breath, her glass door.

"I'll be back before you can miss me," he said.

"I missed you while you were gone today."

"An odd day to miss me."

"A safe day to miss you," she said, looking into the same eyes she'd looked into all those years ago at the duck pond, shadowy eyes that could see the beauty in Afghanistan, eyes that could see things as they were and yet something more.

5

On her second day in charge, she dropped the bag of iPhones and iPads she'd bought for the Fates onto her desk and answered the phone.

"Hey, Cass, it's Gregory. On behalf of the board, we'd like to say congratulations."

"Thanks, I appreciate—"

"We hope you had a good first day because...Well, we know how much you wanted this but..." He cleared his throat.

"But what?" she asked, visualizing Gregory slumped over his too-small desk, twiddling his pencil, his Panama Jack hat pushed back, revealing the baldness it was there to hide.

"Howell is in a bit of a financial situation," he said. "I'm afraid we only have enough money to stay open until the end of the year."

Cass collapsed into her chair. "How can that be? I don't understand."

"The property taxes went up. Actually, everything has gone up. Except for the investments. And we made assumptions based on previous years' incomes and expenditures. Those assumptions proved to be—"

"Why didn't Bev tell me?"

"When she gave us her news, we didn't think...Only the board knows."

"How could you let this happen? How did you not see this coming? How could you not give us a warning?" She pushed back from the desk and stood again, facing the back yard.

"This is your warning."

Overhead, the tall, tall trees—a safe canopy—but too far away, as if a layer were missing. In the past few weeks, it had seemed impossible the fuzziness on the trees would ever turn into large green leaves, but now Cass could see the bare branches of winter.

"How much do we need?"

"Half a million—to make it another year."

Cass closed her eyes. She'd never raised so much as a hundred dollars. "I wanted to be in charge for the Fates, to make their lives bigger, not to spend my time asking people for money."

"Sorry this is falling on you, Cass."

"How long do we have?"

"All I know is the lights go out December 31."

$$\circ \, {}^{\circ} \, \circ$$

Ethan picked up on the first ring. "Hey, babe."

"There's no money," she said.

"No money?"

"Howell House," she said. "There's no money for next year." She stood and then sat, having a hard time being still.

"That can't be right."

She leaned back and swiveled toward the side windows, no longer seeing the trees she knew were there.

"Bev should have told you this months ago."

"She doesn't know."

"Well, the foundation should have told you before you accepted."

"I would have accepted anyway."

"Really?"

"I wouldn't have left the Fates with no one. At least I know I'll try my hardest."

"I'm so sorry. It's hard to believe. How much do you need?"

"Five hundred thousand."

"Half a million—wow. Somebody screwed up."

"Don't say 'half a million.' "

"You just need a few big donors, or one actually."

"I'm worried, Ethan." She stood up and turned to the deck behind her. Like a child, she stomped her foot. "I got what I wanted but without any money for it to last. I've never handled fundraising. I thought I would have more time to learn that part of the job. And I didn't think it would be such an important part."

"You know you can do this, babe," he said. "You're going to be great."

"I had so many plans," she said, sinking back into her chair, staring at the bag of unopened iPhones and iPads.

$$\circ \, {}^{\circ} \, \circ$$

Upstairs, May's door was open. She sat in her favorite spot, a chair facing out the window, her gigantic knitting needles in her lap. Even with daily housekeeping, her room was a mess, but it didn't make Cass feel anxious or as if she needed to clean. With other Fates, Cass would have started picking things up as soon as she opened the door. But May's mess was different, and lovely. It was part of her. And it calmed Cass.

May turned in her direction and smiled, tears streaming down her face.

Cass handed her a tissue.

"Sometimes I can't hold it all inside."

May still looked the same as when Cass first met her—small recessed green eyes, a face that pooled into wrinkles, and familiar white hair soft like the petals of a flower with just enough wisps of it to cover her head, no eyebrows. These days, May had trouble seeing the center of things. Macular degeneration. Light was the only thing that helped.

"I never did like being out there," May said, nodding to the window, still patting her face with the tissue. "At first that didn't make any sense—that I wanted to look *at* it but not be *in* it. My

Harvey was just the opposite. He wanted to be *on* the horse or *in* the water. He didn't just walk on the beach; he dug his toes in the sand. But it doesn't have to make sense, does it?"

"It doesn't," Cass said. May often told her about Harvey digging his toes in the sand.

"People enjoy things in different ways," May said, turning again to the window.

But nothing was happening in the back yard—it was so still it could have been a photo.

"I had a good life," May said finally. "I'm not ready for it to be over. Inside I feel just the same as when my mama called me Cora May and told me to stop spinning, that I was going to make myself sick, but I never did. I can't believe it when I look in the mirror. The first half of my life took place in slow motion. Then I got married and time seemed to stop. Or it seemed irrelevant. I sold real estate, I made dinner, the next thing I knew I was fifty years old."

Cass looked at the window's rectangular panes—still twelve.

"But time is never irrelevant," May said. "It's just hard to see something you're inside of. I should have looked up more."

May told her this almost every day.

"It's a wonderful thing, marriage," May said. "Two people committing to stick together. But it closes doors. It drops you into a container. Before, *anything*. After, *married*."

This was new.

May picked up the needles and the small patch of pink yarn, still staring out the window. "But by making your circumstances fixed, marriage forces change inside you." Her black T-shirt read *Easily Distracted by Shiny Objects*. "Or it busts the container to bits," she said and laughed.

"If you knew then what you know now, would you do it again?"

May turned to her. "But we'll never know before what we know after. It will always be a leap. But, yes, I would do it again."

Huge old oak trees bordered the lot. May's answers weren't

supposed to change. "What do you remember about being a kid?"

"No trash," May said.

Cass relaxed.

"We used everything. Until the paper disintegrated, or the fabric shredded, or the last carrot top had dissolved into the broth. When there were bones, we played with them first and then gave them to the dogs."

Cass leaned against the bed.

"If I were doing it all again, by the way, I'd have a houseful of children."

"Why?"

"They bring the life to the party. They bring the unexpected, the future. But I couldn't have any. Are you sure you don't want any children?"

"Pretty sure." The sky was a clear blue.

"Why?" May dropped the needles and yarn into her lap.

Cass hesitated. "My mother didn't want me. I ruined her life. Then, when I was in seventh grade, I saw a little girl get hit by a motorcycle. And that was that."

"Bless your heart, you were a child yourself."

"Let's read."

"Cass," May said, reaching out. Cass leaned forward and May touched her arm. "Bad things happened to you, but good things can happen, too. Look for the good things. Your heart may surprise you one day." May placed her hands in her lap on top of the needles. "Okay, climb up and get comfortable. Let's read."

Reading to May was how it had all started, and it remained Cass's favorite part of the day. She missed it when they couldn't find time for it—like yesterday. Thirty minutes and then she would go back to the office where there was no money for any of her plans.

Cass dropped her sandals and scooted up. "Page one," she said.

But before she could read the first word, May began from memory. "In the town there were two mutes, and they were always together."

Stretched out on May's bed as if she were a child, listening to the words lift and unfold, Cass looked around this room that seemed bigger than it usually did. She closed her eyes. May's steady, melodious voice grounded and soothed her in a way nothing else could. Cass loved Howell House. It gave her something she couldn't give herself, something not even Ethan could give her—a layer above her.

6

In the light of day, Cass would be able to think straight, she knew that, but it didn't help. In bed now, in the dark, she had only one thought, and it wouldn't let her go. She turned toward Ethan, scooting closer, reaching her arm around him. As he turned toward her, moonlight fell through the windows.

They faced each other on separate pillows.

"You shine, did you know that?" Ethan said, draping an arm across her hip.

She needed more air but wanted to keep his arm where it was. Like a clock hand with a fixed center, she scooted her upper body a little away from him, out of the moonlight, without moving the part of her where his hand rested. But even with several ticks of distance, her heart continued to beat too fast. She was less comfortable, not more, and pulled herself away from him to stand. At the window, she looked past the giant moon to the vast darkness where the lights were minuscule and inconstant. "Someone's going to have to give up too much," she said. "I don't know what we were thinking."

He came up behind her and rested his chin on her shoulder, not leaning against her, not touching her anywhere else, just the bony part of his chin to the bony part of her shoulder. "We were thinking we were worth fighting for."

"I'm afraid," she said.

"Of what, babe?" His words brushed her ear. "Tell me."

She wasn't sure she could say it. Through the top corner of the window, she looked straight at the moon. "I don't want to be the woman who stopped you from going."

He lifted his chin. "You're not stopping me. It's my choice.

I choose you." And he kissed her neck and trailed his mouth along her skin.

She turned to him. "I'm afraid the agreement kills the clearest, strongest part of you."

He took a step away, then turned back to her, as she knew he would.

"Without you, *this me* disappears. Besides," he said, opening his hands, "we may not have even gotten to the clearest, strongest parts yet...of either of us."

"We want different things."

"We want each other."

She was still unsettled and turned back to the window.

But he turned her back to him. "This is middle-of-the-night talk. You need something else to think about." And with one arm, he tightened his grip around her waist and held her close. With his other hand, he began to tuck strands of her hair behind her ear.

When his fingers came close to her face again for what she thought would be another strand, instead, with one finger, he started at her middle part and traced a line down her forehead, her nose, landing above her lips, parting her lips, backtracking to her tongue, and pausing before he continued the same slow motion down her chin, her neck, her chest, stopping between her breasts. Cracking her open.

Then he moved his whole hand sideways.

"What are you doing?" she whispered.

"Searching for your heart," he said, surprising her.

"Love is not the answer to everything." But her knees gave way, gave her away.

He held her tighter, supported her. "Yes," he said. "It is."

7

A couple of days later, Cass made time to call Goodwill about Lois's red shoes. The woman she spoke to said she would see what she could do, and Cass could tell by her questions she really would try to find them. Lois's son could only describe the closets and drawers of stuff he hadn't even gotten to yet. He felt bad, he said, but he had to draw the line somewhere.

Cass wanted to go look for the shoes herself, but somewhere in the stack of papers in front of her were forms for the state that had a deadline. This kind of mess made her feel as if she had no control over anything. She'd just started making piles when Natalie Merchant's voice rang out. Cass looked up. Yes, she thought. Music. And just like that, the papers in front of her seemed less of a chore.

But she heard Ella shouting to turn it down. Atta must have complained. Scooting back her chair, Cass was about to head upstairs when the phone rang. For a second, she just stared at it— the phone had not been her friend lately—but then she picked up.

"Hey, babe," Ethan said. "You didn't answer your cell."

She didn't even know where it was. "It's crazy here today." Outside, the wind was picking up. All around her, tree branches were waving, as if they, too, were trying to get her attention.

"How's it going with the fundraising?"

"Still just sitting with it. But I'm almost ready to start. Any minute. I can feel it."

"That's why I called. I just talked to Setara. Take a look at GoFundMe. She's set up an account to help us raise money for the cameras we need for the Afghans."

Cass tried to listen, and, usually, she could file the Afghan

Woman away, but Setara was with Ethan when Cass was not, in a place where danger was everywhere. The longer Ethan talked—explaining how a GoFundMe account could help her raise money for Howell—and although he never said it, the more she understood.

He was going back.

$$\circ \, ^\circ \, \circ$$

She could barely lift her foot to the next red-carpeted step. In the upstairs hall, Ella was putting clean towels into the armoire. Music was still coming from May's room. Cass knocked and went in. May smiled—a huge smile.

"I don't have to ask what you're listening to," Cass said.

"Over and over again." May was rocking back and forth. "Life is so sweet."

Life is hard was the verse that stuck with Cass.

"I only understand half of what she's saying, but it doesn't matter. It's her voice, the music, the piano, the way it builds. It lifts me up." May closed her eyes.

And Cass closed hers, trying to hear what May heard. At first, she felt weighted to her spot by the plane that would carry Ethan back to Afghanistan and Howell's empty bank account and the piles of paperwork. She did bruise easily...But as she listened, gradually she heard only the music and May's humming and she began to sway and Cass thought how she'd like to turn the music up even louder and for one second, just one flash of chill on her skin, she thought she'd like to twirl around the room. But she opened her eyes and remembered where she was.

8

Ethan had been home a week. While he cleaned up after dinner, Cass read on the sofa. The light went off in the kitchen, and he said he'd be right back, but when she finished her chapter, he still wasn't. At the door to the bedroom, she stopped. He was staring out the windows into the black worry of night.

"Ethan?"

"In Afghanistan, it's already tomorrow," he said, as if he could see it on the glass.

"You want to talk about it?"

He came over and put his arms around her, rubbing her cheek with his scratchy face. "Nothing to talk about," he said, as she laughed.

"Hey, you want to go over to the bar?" she asked, sitting on the bed and slipping her shoes back on. "Hang out with Vee for a while?"

"And watch Singer drool over you?"

"He does not."

"It's Friday night. They'll be packed. I think I'd rather stay here."

"Well," she said, kicking her shoes back off, "let's watch a movie."

After they settled on the sofa, Ethan, with the remote in one hand and her feet in the other, scrolled through the movies. *Amour...Beasts of the Southern Wild...Doctor Zhivago...*

"*Life of Pi?*" he said.

The titles flew by so fast she got dizzy. *The Safety of Objects... Sabrina...The Secret Life of Words...*and from there, her brain short-hopped to Setara. And then that was all she could see, as if

Setara had materialized on the TV in front of them.

Ethan continued to click.

"So how *is* the Afghan Woman?"

"Setara's good." He raised his eyebrows and kept scrolling. "Thanks for asking." When he got to the z's, he looked at her as if to say *What do you want from me?*

"I wish," she said, "that you would say her name in a way that doesn't make her sound like some sort of goddess."

"I don't say her name that way. She's my business partner." But he leaned back, creating too much space between his body and her feet in his lap. And then he set her feet on the floor, collected his empty glass, and stood. He headed toward the kitchen but came back and leaned over her, placing his hands on the back of the sofa on either side of her. "I bought some ice cream today. You want some?"

She shook her head and picked up the remote.

Not only was Setara out saving the world, but she'd had a baby, a little girl, in January. Which had stopped her not at all. She could do anything and everything. Cass squirmed. Most women seemed able to juggle being mothers as well as staying themselves, but Cass couldn't imagine it. And because of Tidal Flats, she had tried to—tried to want children because Ethan did and tried to imagine herself as a mother. But if she ever had a baby, like Samson after his hair was cut, she'd lose her strength, the one good thing her mother had given her. Besides, a baby brought chaos, and she craved control. She just couldn't see it.

The remote felt heavy in her hands. After a few seconds, she put it down and banged her half-full glass of merlot on the end table. She was being ridiculous about Setara. But when Ethan came back and reached for her feet on the floor, she held tight. He could not have her feet.

The next morning, in the early Saturday darkness, Cass picked up her mug of coffee, stuck her computer under her arm, and headed to the chairs in front of the French doors, which she cracked—creating a line of cool morning air she could feel, reminding her of the line of dark she could see under her childhood closet door and the line of light she saw when she was *in the closet* lying under her dresses.

Her fingers rested on the keyboard, but nothing happened. Inside her head, Howell was a mess. She stood. And then she saw it. Two lists—one that put her hopes and dreams for the Fates into order and one that brainstormed ideas to raise money to fuel her hopes and dreams. Everything would go on one of two documents. Get it all out of her and into order.

o O o

Ethan began to clank around the kitchen. She hadn't heard him get up or get in the shower. When he came into the living room, he kissed the top of her head. He would spend the day with his photographs—editing, cataloging, printing.

She reached her hand up for his.

He grasped hers, squeezed once, and let go. "See you tonight," he said. And the door swooshed and clicked.

She raised her head. Out the doors, no trace of darkness. Inside, the rich smell of Ethan's dark roast coffee. She stood and stretched and opened the doors all the way. Leaning on the railing of their French balcony, she took in all the pink and white—the dogwoods sprinkling the city in lace. When Ethan had suggested they move to his apartment in the Westside Provisions District, she'd said *yes* immediately. Virginia Highlands where she had an apartment lacked a vista. Here, she could see farther. There was more air.

This apartment had been so empty—a mattress on the floor, a sofa and TV, the blue wheelbarrow seat. More proof it was meant to be, he'd said. *His* apartment, *her* stuff. After the move, the only thing she missed was looking out her window at that old maple, its fall colors and fullness, and then the bareness of the branches in winter with the empty café patio below.

Atlanta was a city of trees. She'd thought the same thing about Paris, standing at the top of the Arc de Triomphe, when she'd visited with her father the Christmas after her mother died. Now, leaning on the black wrought iron railing, she inhaled the fresh air. Ethan would be back tonight. That was the point of it all. The opening and the closing.

9

Monday mornings, Cass made a special point of checking on each Fate in her own room. Atta was the only one who'd brought a dressing table, and there she sat, braiding her hair. Across the room, on the corkboard over her desk, was a picture of two old women with wrinkly faces. Underneath it said: "We were young and beautiful. Now we are just beautiful." Next to the photos was a white index card with the word *skylark* written on it.

"Is *skylark* your word for today?"

Atta nodded. "Do you know what it means?"

"Isn't it a bird?"

"It is—known for singing while flying. But it's also a verb. It means to frolic or engage in horseplay. Wouldn't hurt you to skylark a bit more."

"I've probably never skylarked in my life."

"Exactly."

Atta was also the only Fate who'd opted for weekly maid service instead of daily, and her bed was already made. No clothes in sight. No piles anywhere. All of her neatly tucked away.

"It always smells so good in here," Cass said.

"Essential oils—lavender and eucalyptus. And I'm not stingy."

"How was your weekend?"

"Six thousand steps each day." She put a rubber band around the end of the braid and added a large silver bangle to each ear. "You can't stop moving. If you do, that's the end."

Atta was leaning into her mirror and applying red lipstick like wings. "The big things always seem to take care of themselves. It's the little things you need to pay attention to—the words, the steps, the lipstick."

○ ○ ○

After shutting Howell's front door at the end of the day, Cass called Vee. They saw each other less when Ethan was home, and Cass missed her. But no answer. She dropped the phone into her bag and relaxed her shoulders, leaving the Fates behind.

An hour later, she was sitting on the rug in front of the fireplace with her computer and the mission of setting up a GoFundMe account when Ethan busted in the front door, dropped his stuff on the wheelbarrow, and lunged facedown onto the sofa. "Apparently I volunteered to be a clown for the Atlanta Children's Diabetes Spring Circus," he said. "Last year. Wheeler's doing, of course, because of his daughter."

Wheeler was a journalist and a photographer. He and Ethan had been in the same class at Georgia State, graduating four years ahead of Cass, and they'd both gone to CNN where Wheeler still worked.

"It's Sunday, the morning after I get back from Boston," he said, rolling onto his back. "I don't know what I was thinking."

"Oh, you'll have fun," she said, lifting herself onto the brick ledge in front of the fireplace.

"Sorry. Did I interrupt you?"

"No," she said. "You're saving me from myself. I can't come up with a name for the Howell House GoFundMe campaign."

"You want to see my costume?" he asked.

"Sure," she said, scooting back to the floor to stack her notes, shut her computer. A paper bag crinkled, and she looked up. Ethan stood there like a bullfighter but holding a one-piece suit, the left half purple and the right half green. "Wow, you're divided."

"There's more," he said, turning back to the bag.

In the calm and hopeful evening light, Cass leaned against the rough brick fireplace and stretched her legs on the rug, on its soft blue swirls that reminded her of a storm. As she watched, her serious husband—in his jeans and worn white shirt, his sleeves rolled up, his blue eyes no longer tired—placed a triangular-shaped purple and green pom-pom on his head and snapped a red plastic ball onto his nose.

○ ○ ○

Toward the end of the week, she opened their front door to round and spongy Wheeler holding a case of beer. After he put it in the fridge, he gave her a giant hug.

"Ethan's on the phone," she said. "I don't think he'll be long. How about a beer?"

"I don't mind if I do," he said, opening the fridge again and twisting the top off one of the ones he'd brought, which he offered to her first.

She shook her head. "How long were you and Gloria married?"

"If I don't mind you asking."

"You love it that I asked," she said.

He raised his beer to her. "Four years. She loved me for a while." He shrugged. "We've made a good life, though, from the pieces." He took a swallow of beer. "But you're a stand-by-your-man kind of girl, aren't you?"

"Way too early to tell."

"Hey, now," Ethan said, coming into the kitchen and shaking hands with Wheeler. "To what do we owe the pleasure?"

"Ethan, old boy," Wheeler said, "I brought you a case of beer as an early 'thank you' for working the clown patrol."

"Well, I'm always happy to drink your beer." Ethan opened the fridge and grabbed one, then leaned against the counter and put his arm around her. "For sure, I'm a stand-by-my-woman kind of guy," he said.

There was a knock at the door. Katie, their neighbor, who was so short and pregnant it looked as if the baby were taking over her entire body.

"I need to print something for work," she said. "And I'm out of paper. I need about twenty sheets?"

"Sure," Cass said, swinging the door open. "I'll be right back."

As she passed the kitchen, she heard Wheeler say, "Another kidnapping. A journalist." At her desk, Cass grabbed the open ream of paper that appeared to have about fifty sheets in it. As she passed the kitchen, she slowed but their voices had turned to whispers.

10

The morning of Wheeler's circus fundraiser, Cass was still in bed when Ethan came out of the bathroom. She yawned, wanting to go back to sleep. He hadn't even gotten home from Boston until eleven, and he'd been keyed up, full of excitement about the exhibit, describing how he'd alternated photos so that inside the door of the gallery, the first photo to the left and to the right was of a person. Whichever way you went, *Unending* began and ended with people. The line of visitors had snaked all the way through the art of Asia, Oceana, and Africa, around the Rotunda, and down the stairs.

Now he was half purple and half green, with that red nose and without a smile. "I feel funny already," he said, heading back into the bathroom.

When Cass was little, she'd never played "dress-up," but she had played "desk" in her room, wearing glasses, swinging her legs, straightening the papers and pens, paying bills.

"You should come with me," Ethan said, and sat next to her on the bed. "There'll be lots of children to practice wanting."

She looked at him, trying to figure out if he were joking. "I'm doing my part," she said.

"I know you are. Just seems like a perfect opportunity. Like to not go is going out of your way."

"I'm in bed. To go would be going out of my way."

"Excellent point," he said, leaning over and kissing her more than once. "Wish I was in there with you."

"Come on," she said, throwing back the covers.

"Wheeler will be here any minute," he said, and pulled himself away.

"Hey," she said, sitting up. "I need to tie the back."

He sat back down.

"I made you a bow," she said, but there was still a three-inch gap that showed his lime green T-shirt.

As he stood, he rested his hand on her leg. Then he picked up his wallet from the wooden bowl. "I wonder what a clown does with his money." His cell phone beeped. "There's Wheeler now." Ethan collected the rest of his clown paraphernalia and said, "Okay, give this clown a proper send-off." He pinched her bottom and honked his horn. "I'll be back in time for supper unless I decide the clown life is the life for me—in which case, come visit me when the circus is in town." He picked up his pillow and threw it at her.

Instead of accompanying him to the door, she slid back under the covers. He still hadn't said he was going back, and like a kid afraid that if she didn't believe she wouldn't get any toys, she hadn't asked.

She tried to imagine him in Afghanistan. There, he wore a beard. There, he dressed in those loose, flowing clothes. But it was all blurry. She could only see him here.

And she *was* doing her part. Right after they got married, she'd bought a journal and directed her thoughts toward children. She'd visited the zoo, stood next to them, spoken to them. In those early days, Ethan might point out how much fun a small family was having at the beach. *See*, he would say. And *yes*, she would reply, *they did* seem *to be having fun*. But she only saw it; she couldn't feel it deep inside. Then she switched her focus to the mothers—watching and listening and talking to them. Finally, she tried making it an intellectual undertaking and read everything she could get her hands on about the wonder and mystery of children.

She wanted to want them for Ethan.

But she just didn't.

She'd thought about pretending—saying she wanted one and seeing what happened. Perhaps if she had mother clothes to put on...

These days, her goal was to not draw any conclusion, to not say out loud or in her head anything final, to remain open for the weeks that remained. But the closer it got to their anniversary, the more she found herself thinking about Ethan's part of the bargain rather than her own. After all, as she'd said more than once to Vee, if he was never done with Afghanistan, she would never have to have a baby.

She picked up her phone.

"Is this the director of Howell House calling?" Vee said.

"Ha ha. How's it going?"

"Ugh—stomach flu."

"Oh dear, can I do anything?"

"Don't mention hamburgers."

"Hope you feel better."

"We'll celebrate when I do. Adios."

Cass slid her computer to the bed. She had to get the GoFundMe account open. But she couldn't come up with a name she thought would *inspire* donations. Maybe if she let go of what she wanted and looked at what she had.

Help Howell House.

It wasn't poetry, but it was a way forward.

"Help Howell House," she typed into the website and clicked and was live, everything else having been in place days ago. Then she clicked on the *Donate Now* button and contributed $100. Her plan was to get the word out to as many people as possible, and she would ask Ella to take charge of the campaign on social media. Next week, letters would go out. After that, an email blast. Building up to the serious stuff—the foundations and potential large donors. She could do this. *She had to do this.*

$$\circ \, ^{\circ} \, \circ$$

Around dusk, she and Ethan set out on foot for Sunday Supper at JCT. Kitchen. Not depending on a car for everyday living was something they agreed on. He hadn't had one since before college; hers stayed mostly in the garage. It had been her high school graduation gift, and she'd always thought she'd trade it in for something smaller when she had extra money. But her parents had given her the Explorer. They'd seen her in it. She had seen them from it. It was a link, a connection. At the time each one had died, she'd hardly kept anything. *Travel light* her father had taught her.

Up ahead, the dirt-red pedestrian bridge extended in an arc over the railbed below. Its design echoed the crossing tracks underneath.

"You look nice," Ethan said. "I've missed how you wear your clothes."

She smiled. "How do I wear my clothes?"

"Like butter," he said, leaning over and kissing her ear. "Like they're irrelevant."

She glanced down. A faded pink tee, a chiffon skirt, sandals.

On one of the tables across from the bar, a family was having a picnic. The baby was crying in the stroller, which the mother was pushing back and forth. Another kid sat in the dad's lap. Still another was smashing potato chips. The dog hid under the table.

"The circus was fun," Ethan said. "It's been a while since I was with little kids for that long. I'd forgotten how the smallest things amaze them. They totally believed I was a clown. I was completely real to them."

"Were you funny?"

"I believe I was, babe," he said, taking her hand.

"How did you even know how to be funny?"

"They painted a big red smile on my face."

"I wish I'd known it was that easy," she said, and flicked him with her jean jacket.

"The tent was packed. Kids and parents and balloons. And they even had an elephant the kids could feed. You should have seen him sling his trunk around a banana. Ate the whole thing—

peel and all."

Last night the elephant wandered India again / and tore the darkness to shreds. One of the five passages her father had underlined. Elephants always made her think of Rumi.

"I just stood there, and kids came up and laughed and hugged me. And the parents would take our pictures. I love kids."

Cass loved Ethan.

And she loved the views from the bridge, especially at dusk—to the right, the old Atlanta Water Works smokestack with faintly lit downtown Atlanta behind it, and to the left, tracks that led into grass and trees and sky. She paused at the top looking away from town.

He came up behind her and rested his chin on top of her head.

She pulled his arms around in front of her and ran her fingers over his knuckles. As she stared at the undeveloped land, she tried to visualize Ethan done with Afghanistan but couldn't do it. What if *he* couldn't do it—what if he couldn't stop going? Ever since Tidal Flats, she'd been thinking of the agreement as something that would keep them together, but as a breeze swirled around them, releasing the overly sweet smell of tea olives, it occurred to her instead that the agreement could be the end of them.

11

The day after the circus, Cass arrived home with a small bag from the market. Ethan was sitting on the sofa facing the door. "Hey," she said, "Wheeler's fundraiser gave me the idea of having a small thing at Howell—balloons, music, games, Fanny's chocolate chip cookies. Saturday morning. I handed out flyers on the way home. And I included the GoFundMe info..." Out of the corner of her eye, she saw Ethan's travel camera bag on the wheelbarrow.

He stood. "I'm going back," he said. "Friday."

"Oh," she said. He wouldn't be here Saturday.

He stepped toward her.

She held up her hand to stop him, and they just stood there miles apart. On the table she'd set that morning—two plates, two napkins, two wine glasses. She let go of the bag of groceries and heard the crack of breaking glass, smelling the wine before she thought of it and turning away from Ethan and the mess and going around the other sofa toward the French doors, which she threw open. She just had to hold on a little longer. Soon, it would always be two.

He squeezed in beside her on the tiny French balcony, but she scooted as far as she could to the right, jamming herself against the edge of the railing.

"It's nothing to get upset about," he said.

"You don't get to decide what I'm upset about."

"Cass—"

"I suspected you were going back. When you mentioned the cameras. But I was hoping you wouldn't." Unable to reach out and touch him, unable to stop him—she wrapped her arms around herself. "I agreed to three years," she said, "and three years isn't up yet."

Then she stepped inside, away from him, to get used to that space between them. Again.

But she could feel him behind her. The front door was so white. Too white. She knocked into a plant.

"Today CNN decided to back us. Which is huge. Now we have money for more cameras, several large printers, and photo paper. They've hired me to document the project. One last trip. Three weeks and I'm done."

She stopped in front of the fireplace.

"These people, they don't have anybody," he said. "They need me."

"But you said you wanted to be with me."

"I do want to be with you." And he added, so quietly she almost missed it, "It's not like your mother."

But she couldn't hear this from anyone else, not even Ethan. It belonged to her. She looked into his still blue eyes. "Don't bring my mother into this."

"Talk to me, please."

She sat on the fireplace ledge. "I don't want you to go," she said, tracing rectangle after rectangle of hard red brick.

He sat across from her. "It's just one more trip," he said.

But that wasn't the way it felt. She picked at the cracked mortar. Everybody in her life always chose *there*. A crumb of mortar popped out, right into the center of the rug, right into the eye of the blue storm. Now there was a hole in the mortar, and when she touched the brick beside it, it shifted.

o ᴼ o

After dinner, Cass called Vee, but she didn't answer. It had to be over two weeks since they'd seen each other. They had talked, but they'd mostly texted, and here was another one. *Eating. See you*

Saturday. Can't wait to catch up!

Cass put her phone down and then picked it up again to check on the Fates, something she rarely did, wanting to leave work at work, but with each day that passed, the money problem seemed more real and their security at Howell, more fragile. When she clicked off, she headed down the hall to the bedroom.

Ethan was pulling a clean gray bottom sheet around a corner of their mattress.

"Do you miss sleeping on a real bed when you're over there?" she asked, picking up the top sheet.

"I never think about it," he said. "But I miss sleeping with you." He glanced at her while he covered another corner. "That, I do think about."

She just stood there watching him on the other side—intently making up the bed.

He straightened. "Actually, I never think about it *anymore*. When I was first over there, I loved the pallets, being so close to the ground. I preferred that."

She tossed him the clean, dark gray top sheet—which he let fall to the mattress.

"Sometimes," he said, "it feels like you don't like the part of me that loves Afghanistan."

She looked at all the gray. "At first, I was afraid of it." She looked over at him. "But I married all of you. I moved in here. With the blue wheelbarrow. And I hung your photos." It sounded, even to her, as if she were trying to convince herself. "I want all of you. I just want all of you here."

He swooshed open the top sheet. A storm cloud descending over the bed. Then he stopped again. "Cass, I need to go one more time. And, yes, I want to go, too. But *you* are the life I want. I don't want a life over there."

The bed was still between them, and something else was coming, she could feel it.

"Sometimes," he said, more slowly this time, "it feels like you're against me. Like Afghanistan is this part of me that you hate."

"Oh, Ethan, sometimes your love of Afghanistan is the thing I love *most* about you. But sometimes—damn it, sometimes I do hate that part. I don't want to, but I do."

His eyes. So, so blue.

She rubbed her chest over her heart. And she felt it like slow motion—his arms reaching for her, their bodies falling to the soft mattress, the safe feeling of his weight on her.

12

They had only hours before he left. With Howell's fundraiser on Saturday, Cass didn't feel guilty taking the day off. She hadn't been to his studio in ages, but it looked no different than it had on their second date. Still no sticky notes, no mugs. A black wire desk that could just fold up and disappear. Nothing except the heft and size of the printer to indicate the permanent presence of anyone.

Westside Atlanta had started as the meat-packing district. Afterward, the warehouses lay empty for years. Ethan's studio, across from their apartment building, was in the old White Provision building, on the third floor that was originally one cavernous empty space. Renovations had turned the floor into three studios, each with a huge window of light.

Ethan turned to a white plastic bin on a card table and removed the lid. The top photo was of Majeed, who had given Ethan the wheelbarrow bench. Her eyes always went first to the glassy sore on his dusty fingers, then to the torn threads of the red vest he was holding. His fifteen-year-old son had been wearing it when he was shot in his own house. He'd wanted to be a teacher.

"I'm going to be okay," Ethan said, touching her elbow and drawing her to him, letting the lid fall to the cement floor. "I'm going to come back to you."

But she thought of her father anyway.

$$\circ \, ^{\circ} \, \circ$$

As he collected what he would need for his trip, she wandered. On a small table by the printer were three 8 ½ by 11 photographs. The top one was of Baquir, Ethan's fixer, who Cass liked to imagine magically knew what needed fixing. Baquir was slight, but tall, like Ethan. This photo, of Baquir carrying a floor lamp across a city street, was one of Ethan's famous *Portraits of Afghanistan*. If she looked closely, the side of Baquir's mouth had just the faintest upturn. Cass smiled. That's why this photo was here. Ethan loved Baquir's sense of humor, which was usually only present at the end of the day when the two of them were alone, but Ethan had caught it in the middle of the day in the middle of the street. In the next photo, also one she'd seen before, Setara was the only woman in a blurry sea of men. And, God, those eyes. This woman knew who she was and what she wanted. And she looked as if she might know who Cass was and what she wanted, too. In every photo, Setara stared straight at the camera, straight at Ethan. Cass turned and looked for him—sitting in front of his computer—and she went back to the photo. Those famous sparkling amber eyes but also something else. These were the eyes of someone attuned to the world, someone who saw things and didn't look away, someone who was in it—for better or worse. Cass scanned the photo— eyebrows, scarf, hair—but nothing fragile. Except Cass felt sure there must be and wondered what it was she couldn't see. She put the photo of Setara down and placed the one of Baquir on top of it.

The last photo in the stack. An eerie blue shape, a yellow blanket across a wheelbarrow, a child bending to the ground. She picked it up and took it over to him. "I've never seen this one."

"It's new, from this last trip." He slipped his arm around her waist. "Baquir and I came across this woman and child in an alleyway. The mother was sitting on some cement blocks and covered, head to toe, in a burka. It rarely happens, but she asked me to take her photo."

Cass looked down at his black curls, his olive skin, the creases across his forehead, his ears that stuck out, the ocean of caring he was capable of.

"Uploading the photo," he said. "I didn't notice anything

unusual. But when I printed it, the woman looked as if she were covered in a shroud, as if she were dead. I had to sit down. I *knew* she was alive underneath."

13

Rounds of cool air from the open French doors pelted her body. No Ethan in the other chair. She had fallen asleep and stood too fast. In her socked feet, she slid down the hallway, bumping over the threshold to their bedroom, grabbing the doorframe to stop herself. Ethan, in his black sweater, with his back to her and black bags at his feet, was packing. Cameras marked with jagged red tape, lenses, cables, and countless other black pieces, all at right angles covering their old quilt. Sleeping during the day made her woozy, and she put her hands to her forehead.

He looked up. "You okay?"

Their feet had been together, on the ottoman between them. "You were gone."

"Not gone. Packing."

"Why didn't you wake me up? I always watch you pack."

"Because you always watch me pack."

But she needed to watch him place things now in this room into those bags that would be with him over there. She perched on the arm of the easy chair.

"Why is there red tape on your cameras?"

"This last trip I picked up the wrong one—first time. Do you have any books for me to take to Setara?"

She reached over to the top of the bookshelf where she collected books for the Revolutionary Association of the Women of Afghanistan. They loaned books to more than five hundred girls. "There aren't many—six, I think."

"Thanks. I got some from work, too."

For Ethan, packing was a numbers game. Everything crammed into three bags for traveling—two carry-ons and one rolling suitcase that he checked. His shiny black hardcover Pelican camera case and his stuffed backpack went with him on the plane. He made sure that if he never saw his checked bag again, he could manage. Over the years, he'd had to function without it twice.

Once he was there, his three bags became five—his collapsible duffel bag that held his body armor and Kevlar came out of his backpack to allow room for a few of the extras that had traveled in his checked bag (like his pocketknife). His padded but flat survival bag (wallet with passport, Afghanis, sim card, press cards, slim medical kit, flat water pouch) also came out of his backpack and went directly onto his back, if necessary easily fitting underneath his larger backpack where he kept one change of clothes (two pairs of socks), his computer, his BGAN satellite modem, his headlamp with red light, his toiletries (including sunscreen, which he never used here), and baby wipes. These bags were his closet and dresser. If he needed to move in a hurry, he was ready.

The rolling suitcase, his jacket, and his boots were already in front of the laundry room door next to her closet. He added his backpack and camera case. The bed was empty now, the piles having disappeared, as she imagined Ethan saw it, in a series of still shots. Seeing nothing but quilt, her stomach dropped.

He checked his watch.

"So, we leave here at seven as usual?" she asked, glancing again at the empty bed.

"Yep," he said, leaning over his dresser, looking at his notes. He picked up his pen and stubbed it on the pad as if it were a cigarette. After he closed his notepad, he threw it over toward his boots and stood there empty-handed. "Just a shower, and I'm ready to go." Still he stood there. Then he leaned down and kissed her—gently as if she might break. "I'm glad I'll only be gone three weeks."

"Hardly worth mentioning," she said, his face inches from hers. She made herself smile.

"I don't like thinking about you here alone." He backed up and sat across from her, on the corner of the bed.

"Then don't go."

"If you had a baby," he said, smiling, "you wouldn't be by yourself. Think about it—a little girl or boy with your smile. And your ears. I don't think I could leave a baby."

Cass felt her next breath like a kick in the chest. Her skin prickled as if it were sunburned. "Ethan," she said, stepping down from the arm and folding into the safety of the chair.

"What?" he said, his hands in front of him, as if she were about to fall.

A baby. Blood was leaving her body.

The baby she'd been trying so hard to want—he would stay for that baby but not for her? Her mind spun ahead to an imagined birth. After the umbilical cord was cut, Cass would shrivel to nothing.

Out the window, the sky was white. She turned to those blue eyes that had always found hers above all the other heads. "Me by myself. I'm not enough?"

He lifted her off the chair and sat with her in his lap, holding her close against his chest. "You know that's not what I meant," he whispered, rubbing her back, his circles growing larger, just like the distance between them.

14

Ethan had been gone twelve hours. As Cass emerged from her building on the way to the fundraiser, the blue sky pressed down. Her whole body felt bruised and achy. Ethan gone and Howell going. Blue, blue, blue.

At nine, Atta, her long braid coiled inside her sequined Sunday black hat, took up her post at the intersection of Howell Mill and Fourteenth, right by the driveway. She held a stack of multicolored flyers with the slogan *Keep Us in a Home*.

As Cass delivered a folding chair, Atta said, "Take that away."

"In case you want a break?"

Atta rolled her eyes. "Standing is my exercise for today."

"Are you sure?"

But Atta had already turned toward a college student in a gray Georgia State T-shirt, jeans, and a black backpack, who seemed shocked at having been spoken to. The boy removed his earphones and accepted a green flyer.

"Your mother will be my age one day," Atta said. "And," as she pointed over to the festivities, she added, "there's a real cute girl over there taking donations. Her name is Ella. Give what you can. We'll take all your change. I know you young people don't like change."

And without saying a word, the guy headed toward Ella, through the gravel parking area that was not deserted today.

Cass carried the chair down the sidewalk to the front walkway, where Lois, surrounded by red balloons, was sporting her dark glasses and a red suede hat that looked too much like a pot turned upside down on her head. Lois smiled—she was always smiling these days—and sat down as soon as Cass unfolded the chair.

On the front porch, Cass had covered a card table in a quilt and topped it with a crystal ball she'd located earlier in the week. This morning, she'd wrapped May's hair in a scarf. For the first time in weeks, May was outside.

As Cass dragged by on her way back inside, May said, "Sit. I'm going to start with you."

Cass shook her head.

"If I can sit here, you can sit there."

Cass sat.

"Give me your hands."

Cass placed each one on the table, palm down.

May's blue-ribbed hands turned Cass's smooth hands over. "Your palms are soft," May said.

Which made Cass think of Ethan's callused ones.

May closed her eyes. When she opened them, she said, "At all times, far more is happening on your behalf than your physical senses can reveal."

"What?" Cass said.

"That is all. The Madame has spoken."

"You seem real."

"I am real."

Cass smiled and stood, fine on the outside but on the inside, unnerved rather than reassured. She was over here, Howell was over there, and Ethan was too far away.

○ ○ ○

Ella's boyfriend was a local DJ, and he would broadcast from the parking lot until noon—giving them a wider potential donor group. And music. Which changed everything.

Around 9:30, Wheeler arrived in his clown suit and for two hours, he walked back and forth on the sidewalk. Fanny in her white chef's apron kept the homemade cookies coming, and Ella stayed at the table with her computer, taking donations. "I can feel the energy, Cass," Ella said, in her glasses that were accessories only. "You're doing it."

Cass looked around at May and Atta and Lois. Ella was right. They were not all smiling, but their faces were animated. And although each was now sitting, including Atta, each was still out here participating. Cass took advantage of the calm to spin through the Westside area handing out flyers that included the GoFundMe information. As she approached the White Provision building, she sighted the large window of Ethan's empty studio and paused. She hadn't answered his calls. She didn't know how to respond to what he'd said about being able to leave her but not a baby. What she did know was that it wasn't an argument for having one.

At noon, Vee swooshed in wearing purple leggings, a yellow dress, and flip-flops. With a portable speaker, she would keep the music going.

"I'm so glad to see you," Cass said. "It's been ages." Vee looked thinner, and pale. The shards of her jagged haircut stood out. "Are you okay?"

Vee waved her hand in front of her face. "Did he get off?"

Cass nodded. It wasn't the right time or place to go into details. The wind gusted, and she looked around, making sure everything that needed to be tied down was. When she looked back at Vee, her bangs had blown over to the side, and there was a scar above her left eye that Cass had never noticed before. "When—"

"Cass," Ella called.

"Go," Vee said. "We'll catch up later." But a little after two, she waved at Cass across the parking area and was gone.

When they closed down at three, they had raised just over $5,000, their goal for the day, doubling what they'd already raised on GoFundMe.

"Only $490,000 to go," Ella said. She closed her computer, stood, and folded her chair.

"We'll find a way," Cass said, not knowing if they would and continuing to sit there, trying to absorb the reassuring sturdiness of Howell's red brick.

15

In her apartment after the fundraiser, it was so quiet she swallowed, thinking maybe her ears were the problem. It was also dark—the blue day having given in to gray skies—but when she flipped on the kitchen light, she felt as if she were about to be interrogated. In the fridge, not much of anything. Mayonnaise, mustard, butter, a few jars of jam. Things that went with other things. Only the other things were absent. It was an emptiness that, after just twenty-four hours, was starting to grow mold. She tossed the mayonnaise.

This kind of alone was a different place than the alone she'd lived in before she knew Ethan. Instead of still, she was restless. Instead of satisfied, she wanted things. Her dinner of chips and cottage cheese was no longer enough. She should make a grocery list for tomorrow. Fresh bread. Milk and eggs. The sort of things people counted on.

In the den, Ethan's photos commanded the room—above, and on each side of, the fireplace—but the only time she noticed them anymore was when he wasn't here. Six of her favorites framed in three different sizes, all in the plain black frames he used for his exhibits. The two largest, which she'd hung next to each other over the fireplace, were two photos of young girls—each eight years old, according to Ethan. Each with dark eyes, dark hair. The one from Kandahar wore a rose-colored dress and scarf; the one from Herat, a gray dress and scarf. The longer Cass looked at the girls, the more she could see. The one in the pink scarf was independent and stronger than she yet knew; the one in gray, determined to survive. All the photos except these two were of more than one person, and all the photos except one of the girls were bursting with color. But what was true of all six was that in none was there any sign of movement. Ethan took so many photos of people walking, riding on bicycles, people on trains, on donkeys, pushing wheelbarrows. People in motion. People unaware of his camera. But Cass wanted to study the people who'd paused for him, who'd stared into the camera, and she wanted to know what they'd been thinking as he had pressed down on the shutter.

Cass was proud of his photos—she'd fought to hang them—but when Ethan had returned from Afghanistan and seen the photos framed on the wall, they had both stood there staring, neither of them saying what they both were surely thinking—that his most famous photo was not among her favorites. That of course *The Afghan Woman* wouldn't be.

Standing here now, Cass knew framing these photos had been a mistake. Every time she noticed them, the thought that overshadowed all others was about what was not here instead of what was.

$$\circ \; {}^{\circ} \; \circ$$

As the world around her began to darken, she made sure the front door was locked. Then she turned on the lamp by her bed and turned out the lamp in the den and the light in the kitchen. Burrowing in—her ritual when Ethan wasn't here. She preferred to hang out in the bedroom, where, out the window, cars were still stopping and starting on the connector. Other people were turning on lights here and there—pinpoint sparkles against the black screen of night. Once in her pajamas, she pulled back the covers, careful not to look at the empty side of the bed. Just yesterday, Ethan had been here.

$$\circ \; {}^{\circ} \; \circ$$

The archaic landline on her desk rang out. Unless there was a problem, Ethan called at eleven, seven thirty the next morning over there. If he couldn't talk, he let the phone ring only once. That way, at least Cass would know he was okay.

A second ring meant he could talk, and she could pick up if she wanted. There was the second ring.

She put her book beside her on the bed and watched the clunky, black phone. If it rang three times, he wanted to talk to her. There was the third ring.

Now the phone was silent, as if it had never rung at all. And she reached her hand out and placed it on the receiver, already regretting not answering.

$$\circ\ ^\circ\ \circ$$

Later, in the darkness, she turned face up and extended her arms down her body. Trying to sleep was speeding her up, not calming her down. She turned on the light.

On a high shelf in the back of her closet, in a shoebox of old prescription bottles she'd brought from her apartment, she found the Xanax from after her father died. It was expired but half full. The pill felt familiar and made her hand feel small.

When she'd gotten her period the first time, her mother had come into the bathroom holding a bottle of Midol. She'd sat on the edge of the tub and told Cass about sex and birth control. She said *her* mother had told her if she wanted to have sex, she needed to get married. "But that's not true," her mother said. "You don't have to get married to have sex. And children are not for everybody. Being a mother is a choice you make. And there are other choices."

Sitting on the toilet, Cass had stared at her mother, who wasn't looking at her but off somewhere. Cass's best friend, Dee, had gotten her period a whole year earlier in the town they lived in when they were only in fourth grade. Dee's mother had fixed her a special dinner.

"I didn't want children," her mother said. "But I didn't think ahead. I didn't plan. And I wasn't strong enough to say 'no.' I wasn't strong enough to do what was needed." Her mother's head sank, and Cass noticed how dirty her hair was.

When her mother's head rose again, so did her voice. "Knowing these things will make you strong. Will make you stronger than me."

Cass hunched over, her stomach cramping.

"I wanted to be an artist," her mother said. "The next thing I knew, my clothes had spit-up on them, and I was changing dirty diapers. I was watching you. All day. Your father is never here." She looked at Cass as she pulled the two sides of her shirt together at her throat. "The part of me that wanted to be an artist dried up. Shrank to the size of a raisin."

Cass waited.

"A raisin," she said again, as she always did.

"At the beginning," her mother said, and she stood and leaned against the bathroom wall, "when it was just me and him and love—that's how it's supposed to be."

Her words sounded watery and dreamy.

Only then did her mother untwist the cap on the bottle she'd been holding and give Cass one Midol. She ran water in the Cinderella cup that had been in that bathroom as long as Cass could remember.

"Love is what you want. Not kids." She held the cup out.

And Cass swallowed the pill.

o ° o

The next afternoon, Cass flopped on the sofa. Maybe she *should* have a baby. Maybe that's all she was good for. Which shocked her into sitting. She shook her head as if it were an Etch A Sketch. Out the French doors, the sky was devoid of color. Inside, the hum of the fridge. *Emptiness...don't think / you must avoid it. It contains*

/ *what you need!* Another of her father's underlinings. Rumi and her father were like bookends—Rumi being born in Afghanistan; her father dying there.

In the bedroom, she picked up their silver-framed wedding photo, the one where she was floating away from Ethan and he was reaching for her. That dress—the way it hugged her body at the top and flared out into ruffles at the bottom, the ruffles like music she knew existed somewhere inside her, the dress like hope. When she'd tried it on in the store, even before she looked in the mirror, she'd known it was *her* dress. The day of their wedding, Wheeler had taken the photo, capturing forever that moment of Ethan reaching for her in that dress full of hope.

Lately, there had been too much thought and not enough sound—Cass had missed the music. But instead of turning on a song, she moved to her desk and opened Skype. Usually she waited for him to call her, but if he could reach for her, she could reach for him.

But he didn't answer.

Which she'd known was likely to happen and yet she felt herself sinking.

Then her computer rang out, and she accepted the call.

"Oh, babe," Ethan said, one beat after his face appeared on her computer, a little dark and blurry but otherwise intact. "I'm sorry. That wasn't the way I wanted to leave."

"I know," she said, relaxing finally. She had been pushing him away, which trapped him under her skin, which only trapped her own voice even farther down. She ran her fingers through her hair and tried to smile into the screen. "It's late there. After midnight."

"We've been cooped up here since we arrived. Gunfire all around the city."

Her body tensed. "Gunfire?"

"The spring season of fighting began earlier than expected. We haven't been able to get out there with the cameras yet. I'm not sure when we can. I may need to stay longer than I thought."

She exhaled and sat back in her chair, causing a creak that sounded as if the chair were about to break. "E, you say you don't want anything between us, but you keep putting things there. I don't need to worry about the baby thing. You'll never give up Afghanistan, will you?"

"Cass, I—"

Behind him, the door opened, and there was Setara wrapped in a towel.

We've been cooped up here since we arrived.

Long dark hair shimmering over bare arms, bare legs, Ethan turning at the sound of the door, those famous eyes, sparkling amber jewels, looking straight at Cass, eyes that took what they wanted, eyes that apologized for nothing. The video disappeared. As if Setara and Ethan had suddenly vanished from Earth.

Setara and Ethan.

Cass shivered. Staying small, she closed her computer although there was no need. He was gone. She ticked forward ever so slightly, turned off her cell, and unplugged the landline. She was no longer in this room but locked away in a childhood room where she sat waiting for the prince who wasn't there to somehow magically save her. In her hard-backed desk chair, she waited, while the light went from blurry to impossible to deep and dark.

16

It took her a minute before she connected the too-bright sun with the darkness of the night before. As she sat up, she shaded her eyes. Still in her clothes and lying on top of the covers, her mouth was sour. The image of Setara's long black hair like the tentacles of an octopus, and the towel, and Ethan, the two of them together on the screen—it all came rushing back and she needed a hard surface. She stood. Brushing her teeth, she wanted to slide under the water and let it wash her away. But more than a shower, she needed to get out of here. She grabbed a washcloth, ran a corner of it under the faucet, and swiped at her eyes, trying not to look at any other part of her, and certainly not at the whole of her.

Back in the bedroom, there was even less air than there had been a minute ago. Flip-flops and a black zip jacket on top of her leftover T-shirt and jeans. A visual sweep of her desk, left to right, and into her messenger bag purse went her stack of notes, her still-turned off computer and charger, and Rumi. And when she picked up Rumi, there underneath was the book Vee had given her for her birthday the year before—May Sarton's *Journal of a Solitude*, where every meeting with another human was a collision and Cass knew what that felt like—and in that book went, too. She grabbed her phone and charger. Over her head went her purse. In the kitchen, she added a bottle of water.

When the door slammed behind her, she exhaled. Safe.

Dropping her keys into her purse, she headed down the hallway but sensed movement on her right. A door opening. Katie's door.

"Oh, my God," Cass said before she could stop herself.

"I know," Katie said. "I'm huge. Past due."

"Does it hurt?"

"The little one's doing gymnastics in there. Feel this." Katie reached toward Cass's hand.

Cass scooted away to push the elevator button. "Sorry. Meeting someone."

"I need you to zip me up. Tom's not here, and I have to go out. That's why I opened the door. I was hoping those footsteps belonged to you."

Cass glanced toward the elevator but then jerked toward Katie who had already turned around. Nothing but an expanse of skin. She had been little like Ella—where had all this flesh come from? Cass elbowed her purse behind her and with her left hand scrunched the flowery fabric together, zipping with her right. The elevator pinged open. Cass focused. Zipping Katie into a life she would never be able to get herself out of.

○ ○ ○

The coffee shop was packed at eight on Monday morning, but Cass came in as a guy at the back corner table stood. Work. Don't think; just call in sick.

Her computer was off but now open, the black screen staring at her. She shut it. *Two hands. Hold onto your coffee with two hands.*

She couldn't make it add up. Ethan wouldn't do what it looked like he was doing. Her stomach lurched, and she knew she should eat something. Coffee on an empty stomach—no dinner the night before—was not a good idea. Back at the counter, waiting in line, her eyes locked on the lemon pound cake Ethan loved. Perhaps if she ate it...

"Can I help you?"

Cass felt a little woozy.

"Are you okay? You look really pale. Maybe you should sit down." A barista she'd never seen before was wearing a baseball cap. Not the Braves but the Rockies. Her dark hair was gathered to the side in a ponytail that wrapped around her neck.

"Do you have toast?"

"Just the breakfast sandwiches. I like the sausage one."

Cass ordered the sausage one and dropped the sausage into the trash on the way to her seat as she took a bite of the English muffin. More people came in, so many people she faded into the crowd, so many she dwindled to insignificance. Still she wanted more. Three more people, she decided, and she could turn on her computer. Her phone would be harder. His voice on voicemails she was sure he had left. A bite of bread. A little coffee. Too hot. A few minutes later, when the third person came in, he was followed by three friends, as if the universe had known she might drag it out. The parade left her no choice, and she tapped the broken circle to start her Mac.

Five emails—she counted without reading words. She raised her head. Four guys, Georgia Tech students by their T-shirts, were saying, "Man" over and over again, shuffling around, hands in pockets, one of them the guy from the fundraiser, the one Atta had sent to Ella. The door opened again. A girl wearing very short shorts. Cass opened the most recent email, the one from a few hours ago. *Please, please call me.* And before she could register how she felt, a pregnant girl opened the door, and Cass opened another email. *Nothing's going on.* Maybe the girl wasn't pregnant. Maybe it was just the jacket she had on. Maybe Ethan didn't love her. Maybe he only loved her when he was here.

The college guys all had their coffees and were watching the girl in shorts bend over the cold drinks in the glass case, except for the fundraiser guy who glanced at Cass but looked away before she could raise her hand in acknowledgement. When the door opened the next time, an older couple came in, wearing matching bike shorts and hanging all over each other, as if trying to prove something. She opened another email. *Cass, it's been hours. Babe, call me. This is NOT a problem.*

She took hold of her computer with two hands. The second email Ethan sent. *Cass, I've tried to call you again and again. I've called the house, your cell. It was just a shower situation. Call me please.* And the first one. *Cass, Setara's shower is broken. Call me back. I love you.*

Knowing Setara's shower was broken didn't make her feel any better. Cass had seen her eyes, her shiny black hair sliding down her body. Her bare legs and arms. The towel. Too easy for what wasn't supposed to happen to happen.

Cass closed her computer. Her stomach twisted and knotted. There was still her phone to deal with. Starting to feel cornered again, she stuffed her things into her bag. Once outside, with the red brick of the coffee shop at her back and the wide open arms of the sky in front of her, she turned on her phone—but only long enough to ignore the texts and listen to the five voicemails, the last one just the sound of no one there.

Cass, don't shut me out. Her shower's broken. Nothing is going on.

I'm just going to keep calling.

Cass, it's me.

I love you.

Click.

17

Cass circled the coffee shop, then expanded to circle the block, and then circled the blocks that contained Westside. When she passed Howell House on the other side of the street, she imagined moving in there, but as much as she loved the Fates, that just made her feel sadder, as if part of her had disappeared.

She needed to get a hold of herself. He said it was just a shower situation. That made sense. She knew she should believe him. She kind of *did* believe him. But she couldn't get Setara out of her head.

Hard cement beneath each footfall, the slap of the plastic flip-flop against her heel, the smell of coffee. As Cass passed the library, she thought it was time to try being inside again, to see how that felt. Perhaps Vee and the quiet of the spaces and the calm of the books would enable her to slow down, to stop moving, and finally to go home.

But Vee was helping someone at a computer, and when she waved, Cass turned and bolted out the front door. In the back corner of the lawn was a bench, and she sat. Next to the bench, a sculpture of three stacks of books, each stack a different color—orange and blue and green—each stack teetering, all the books forever about to crash onto the lawn.

The heavy door clanked open behind her. "Hey," Vee said. "Why aren't you at work?"

Vee was standing there, hovering above Cass in the harsh light of day, and Cass couldn't remember why she'd wished for her, why she'd imagined telling her about the slow-motion feel to Ethan's movements as he turned to see Setara behind him, as if she would talk about something bad that had happened to her.

"You hoo? Anybody home?" Vee sat down.

Her hair had blue streaks in it. Cass pointed.

"I needed a change," Vee said. "Why aren't you at work?"

"I needed a break," Cass said.

"I hear you, Sister." Vee angled her head back and closed her eyes. "It feels so awesome out here. I love spring. The sun announcing itself, demanding attention. Everything fresh and new. Hopeful."

It was evening in Kabul, and Ethan had spent a whole day not having heard from her. "It makes me crazy when people call him '*The Afghan Woman* guy.' "

Vee's head fell back into place.

"She's a rebel," Cass said. "Apparently."

"I used to own a gun," Vee said. "Shooting was on both my lists."

"A gun?" Cass stared at Vee.

Vee nodded. "It's not all that hard to be a rebel."

"Did you know how to use it?"

"I learned."

Cass had no idea what to say and picked up her bottle of water. For a moment, the image of a gun had knocked the image of the towel out of her brain.

"I kept feeling like it was going to go off." Vee said, "I'm glad I don't have it anymore. Now I want an Airstream trailer."

A little after six, after spending the afternoon in the library basement staring at an open book, Cass let Vee talk her into going for a beer. They wove through the maze of tables in the bar to the counter. Singer nodded as they sat down. The first time she'd come to the bar with Vee, years ago, Singer had been here—the artist bartender, sketching people's faces on the back of cardboard coasters. His mother was Vee and Dillon's next-door neighbor.

And he was the one who'd told Vee about the job at the library. *Singer*—thick, auburn hair, a sprinkling of freckles, and golden.

Cass's face broke into a smile, which surprised her—his ability to pull her out of herself. "How's it going?" she asked.

"I'm living the dream," he said, standing in front of them and opening his hands as if what more could he ask for. "Beer?"

Cass nodded.

"Absolutely," Vee said. "Since I'm living *in* a dream."

He rubbed Vee's arm, which Cass had never seen him do before, and then he swept to the other end of the bar—in his jeans, hunter green sweater, and running shoes.

"He seems like a movie star," Vee said. "As if the light is always shining on him."

"Definitely," Cass said, and turned to Vee. "Did the gun make you feel safer?"

"It didn't actually," Vee said. "It was more like my fear had turned into a thing—a dangerous thing."

Cass glanced up at the basketball game on the silent TV.

"We need something to take your mind off Ethan," Vee said.

Cass continued to stare at the screen. "Who said my mind's on Ethan?" After all, he was probably asleep. Or maybe not. She looked into her glass. She hated basketball.

Singer delivered their beers and a water for Cass, smiled at each of them, and drifted off, popping the counter with the palm of his hand.

Cass drank her beer as if it were water, and when she set the glass down, almost half was gone. Vee, however, was biting into the orange that came with the beer as if it were a lime, and she tossed back a slug of beer as if it were a shot of tequila. Not that Cass had ever done a shot of tequila, but she had seen other people do it.

"The old card catalogs," Vee said, pursing her lips. "The cabinets and all the little cards. Ever wonder what happened to them?"

Cass raised her eyebrows.

"Didn't think so. No one ever asks about them. I think that's sad. Our giant cabinet is at the bottom of the stairwell in a closet. And the baby four-drawer one is upstairs in the children's section. While I was up there today, I opened one of the drawers."

"And?" Cass drank another mouthful, then fiddled with her knife and spoon.

"Recipe cards."

"Recipe cards?"

"Tapioca pudding," Vee said, seeming to shrink a tad. "Easy lasagna."

"Why is the thing even in the library?"

"As history, I guess. I don't know, the cards always seemed..."

"Trapped," Cass said, drinking more beer. The alcohol was opening her pores. Her internal pressure was dropping. She needed to drink faster, and she took another swallow as if it were something good for her.

"I was going to say *alive*," Vee said. "As if they might magically come to life at night after I lock the door. But with the recipes—"

"We should free the cards," Cass said, turning to Vee. "Bust into the library and free them."

Other people crowded the bar, talking loudly. Cass turned her glass up, swallowing every last drop of beer, something she wasn't sure she'd ever done before. And something she didn't think she'd ever do again either. Too warm and bitter at the bottom.

She plunked her empty glass down, nodded to Singer when he looked in her direction, and said to Vee, "Ethan told me before he left that if we had a baby, he didn't think he'd ever want to leave."

"Whoa, are you kidding me?"

Cass picked up the second beer without realizing Singer was still setting it down. Beer spilled all over her hand, and she licked it off. When she looked up, Singer was watching her. She took a drink, and cold burst down her throat. Vee's phone buzzed and she looked at it, then at Singer, then she turned it over. But not before

Cass saw that it was Dillon calling.

As Singer started toward the other end of the bar, Cass slung her beer on the counter as if she were in some sort of western. "Wait a minute," she said, a little too loud, ignoring the puddles she'd created.

Singer stopped where he was and looked at her.

"I'm starving."

Singer grinned. Vee looked at her.

"What?" she said.

"You're not usually so, uh, direct," Vee said.

"I think I forgot to eat lunch."

"I think one stupid beer went to your head," Vee said.

"Pasta would be the best thing," Singer said, "and the quickest. They're backed up in there."

"Two pastas," Vee said, and Singer headed to the kitchen.

"I'm not drunk on one beer."

"Okay," Vee said, taking a sip of her first beer that was only half gone. "Did you know you're kicking the bar over and over, about a kick a second?"

"Sorry," Cass said, placing her hand on her leg. She took another huge gulp. Maybe she *should* try something in a little glass to throw back.

"Men," Vee said. "Jeez, so many reasons to be in here drinking." And she, too, took a big, long, drink.

All around them, people were ordering and others delivering. Singer was shaking martinis. There was music in the air. Returning to the apartment seemed possible.

"Ethan made me feel...small. Like a child again. I was never good enough for my mother. She didn't want a baby. She told *me* never to have a baby. Blah, blah. And then seeing that little girl hit by the motorcycle and her little dog licking her face out in the street. And now this. Definitely, no kids for me."

"Oh, Cass."

"But I hated that I let him leave that way. It took me two days to get over it." She took a sip of beer in between each sentence. "So last night I called him. And while he and I were skyping, Setara came into his room. Wearing a towel. Nothing but a towel."

"My God," Vee said, turning to face Cass and putting her hand on Cass's arm. "Why didn't you tell me? No wonder."

Cass set the beer on the counter as her body took over, drawing in a huge amount of air and letting it out slowly. Her shoulders dropped back into place. She felt better, but she didn't like talking about things. Unless maybe she did. Unless maybe, before Vee, she'd never had the right person to talk to.

"A red-and-white striped towel, to be specific."

"Bartender," Vee yelled to Singer. "Another round."

"I've always wanted to say that."

"Stick with me," Vee said.

"I think I will."

Vee smiled. "Maybe we want something stronger than beer?"

"I think we just want a lot of beer."

Vee laughed. "That'll work." She rubbed Cass's arm, like Singer had rubbed hers. "But really, are you okay?"

"I don't know. I didn't know how I was going to make it through the day, but I've almost done that."

"Why was she in his room?"

"That's the thing. We 'suddenly' lost connection. I turned my cell off, unplugged the landline, and took a Xanax. This morning I had texts, voicemails, emails. He said there was nothing to it."

"You don't believe him?"

"I want to, but something doesn't feel right. Maybe it's just her."

"It's interesting," Vee said, "what you don't know about people."

Throughout the bar, music was playing. In her lap, Cass's hands were balled into fists, and she opened them. Singer slid in with the round Vee had ordered. On the fresh, cold mug, Cass lined up her thumbs, one next to the other, around the hard, thick, glass.

"I've been on her side," Vee said, "ever since I saw Ethan's photo of her. I never would have thought that she wouldn't be on ours."

"Since I've known Ethan, she's been 'those eyes.' But now she's a whole body."

"So what the fuck was she doing in your husband's room wearing only a towel? What did he say?"

"That her shower was broken."

"The old 'broken shower' excuse."

Cass looked at her.

"Sorry," Vee said. "Too soon."

"When Ethan and I got married, we had this old hippie minister, a friend of Ethan's mother. During the ceremony, he said the secret of marriage was a willingness to wade through the river of forgiveness. That phrase came back to me today while I was at the library. I didn't think much of it during the ceremony. Back then, I thought the secret of marriage was love."

"I always thought the secret of marriage was sitting down with a glass of wine at the end of each day and talking. It worked for my parents."

"When he was here, it was wonderful. Just like always."

"It's Afghanistan. Odds are her shower was broken."

"I don't know what's worse—to think she goes into his room like that all the time or to think she might have done it on purpose, knowing we were skyping."

"We know she's gorgeous. And that nobody's perfect. She must be a bad person."

"But she's had a horrible life."

"Is she married?"

"Yep. Ethan says she paid her husband to marry her so she could have more freedom. And she just had a baby, a little girl."

"Well, there's an idea—hiring our husbands. Then we could fire them."

"Apparently Setara's not interested in love." But Cass didn't used to be interested in love either.

"Ethan loves you."

"I know."

Vee sitting beside her was helping. Cass felt her eyes relax—as if they were letting her know she could trust them, that it was okay to relinquish control, to let them operate on their own, naturally. "He told me this would be the last trip."

"But?"

"No 'but.' "

Vee looked at her.

"A little 'but.' It's hard to believe."

"The only words Dillon ever said to me that I believed were that he loved me."

Cass turned to face her friend. "Sorry I've been so preoccupied with myself."

"You can talk about yourself all night for all I care. I'm just happy you're here. Keep it coming."

"Ethan's never not followed through on something he's agreed to."

"Dillon has never followed through on anything the entire time I've known him. I married him because I loved him. I didn't know that wasn't enough."

"Vee, are you okay?"

She nodded, but something was off.

"So, what if he won't stop going over there?" Vee said.

"Doesn't Dillon want to see you after work?"

"All Dillon wants after work is a drink. Then he's drunk."

Cass eyed the beer in front of her. "But I need to loosen up. I want to be more like you. I want to be a wild warrior."

"Right on, Sister," Vee said, and they clinked glasses. "What made you fall in love with Ethan?"

"He made me feel special. While we were on a date, he'd ask me out for the next one. The first time he went to Afghanistan after I met him, I didn't know how long he'd be gone. He had no idea either. Actually, he usually has no idea, but I didn't know that then. I came home from work one day, turned the corner on the landing, and found him leaning against my door, asleep, his three bags beside him. And right that second, my heart busted through the wall I'd built around it. I can see him now, through the light gray bars of the banister, his black curls falling into his face, his black sweater, his jeans. He had come straight to my house from the airport. He was waiting for *me*."

"Swoon."

"What made you fall for Dillon?"

"He was so hot."

"Lookout," Singer said, holding two giant bowls of pasta and wiping the area in front of them clean with one swoosh. He set the bowls down and said, "Something's missing." He reached under the counter and brought out a candle, which he lit, dropped into a glass, and placed between them. Singer's hands. Cass loved his hands. He couldn't talk without moving them. And the garlic and tomatoes were steaming, vapor rising from the bowl, blurring the thick red sauce. A fancy silver grater appeared in front of her. "Say when," Singer said. But Cass just waited until he quit turning the handle that looked as if it were a toy in his strong hands. She loved cheese. She could never get enough.

18

In the elevator to their apartment, Cass leaned her head back and closed her eyes, but the tiny space began to spin. She opened her eyes, and now she didn't appear to be moving at all. The button. She hadn't punched the button with the three on it. At the door to their apartment, she dropped her keys twice before she got the key in the lock, and when she finally got the door open, the landline was ringing. She ran to the bedroom and lifted the receiver. "What the hell, Ethan?" she said. "What's going on over there?"

"Nothing. I'm sorry. This house we've rented is falling apart. Her shower doesn't work. She was supposed to wait until I went back downstairs. I should have locked my door."

"How could you let that happen?" she said, kicking the bedpost.

"A boundary is a challenge to Setara. She does things to prove she can."

Cass sank into the bed.

"Oh, babe," he said. "The last thing I want is to hurt you."

This was Ethan. If she didn't believe him, everything fell apart. *Tidal Flats.*

The exhaustion of the last twenty-four hours overcame her, and she crawled under the covers, wedging the phone under her chin. He promised to stay on the line until she fell asleep, his voice holding her steady as she let go of that red-and-white towel.

19

A week after the towel situation, Cass was sitting at the bar, a full beer in front of her, when Singer came toward her pouring another one. Then Vee plopped down beside her, and he handed her the glass.

"How does he know when you're about to walk in the door?" Cass asked.

"I text him."

"Damn, I was thinking magic. Bad day?"

"Two kindergarten classes this morning. Not one. Two. And just now this library association thing, and ev-ry-bo-dy had a problem with something."

"Ha," Cass said.

Vee's phone buzzed, and she reached for it. "Fuck," she said, dropping it in her purse. "Sorry. Incredibly sorry. I've been looking forward to seeing you all day, but I have to go." She took a huge sip of beer, threw down a ten, and squeezed Cass's arm.

"That was quick," Singer said. "Is she coming back?"

Cass shook her head and reached into her purse to find her wallet. When she looked up, Singer had collected Vee's glass and the money, and was standing in front of her. "You don't have to run off, too, do you?"

She glanced out the windows into the vacant dark.

"I get off at ten," he said. "I'd be happy to walk you home."

Lonely, lonelier, loneliest. Her progression through the day.

"Okay, cool," she said, putting her wallet up. In all these years, he'd never offered to walk her home, but she wasn't sure she'd ever been here later than Vee before. Over the next twenty minutes, he checked on her several times. At ten, she told him she'd wait outside.

The April night fell on the cool side, but she unzipped her jacket, wanting fresh air. She held onto a bench and tilted her head back, soaking up the inky blue sky and the sprinkling of stars. Alive, that's how she felt.

The door opened. "Feels great out here, doesn't it?" Singer said.

"It's weird to see you on the other side of the counter." She turned toward her apartment.

"Out of my cage."

"All the time I've known you, and I've never seen you out in the wild."

His smile grew wide. He stuck his hands in his pockets.

Ahead, illuminated street lamps lit the way. She wasn't sure if there was a moon or not, and she didn't want to look up, didn't want to search for it. Walking beside Singer felt more than comfortable—easy and automatic—as if she did it every day.

"Nice of you to walk me home," she said.

"I don't like being by myself either," he said. "Neither does Vee. I guess that's why she's always at the bar. Other than Dillon, she has no family here. Unlike me."

"Right, your mother."

"And brothers and sisters—six of us. We're always just showing up at each other's place. How about you?"

"No one except Ethan."

"No parents?"

She shook her head. "Both died a while ago."

"Damn. Sorry."

"My mother, my first year of college. And a year later, my father. In a plane crash in Afghanistan. Operation Enduring Freedom."

"Your father was in Afghanistan, too—wow. What about Ethan? Does he have family here?"

She shook her head. "Just a hippie mother in Big Sur."

"Brothers, sisters?"

"We're only children, both of us."

Singer opened the door to her building, and she turned to thank him.

"I'm going to deliver you all the way to your apartment."

"You don't need to do that."

"I'm not coming in," he said, grinning, "even if you beg me."

Inside the elevator, they stood apart. He watched the numbers change, and she watched him. When the elevator opened onto the third floor, he followed her out but stopped in front of the huge pink ribbon.

"Somebody had a baby girl, I see."

"Katie." Cass stopped, too. "Every time I walk by, I think of all the baby toys and diapers and crying and exhaustion and forever of it, as if there's no way back from what's behind that red door."

"I was thinking of the joy," he said. "But you're probably right about the other stuff."

Joy. A word that seemed foreign. More like a memory, the name of someone or something she'd once known but so long ago it wasn't even on the tip of her tongue, nor did she know what letter it started with.

"Here I am," she said, putting her key in the lock. She could feel Singer backing away.

"Have a good night," he said, heading to the elevator.

"Oh, come in, will you? Have a glass of wine, or a scotch, or whatever it is you drink. I'm sick of this empty apartment."

He stopped where he was. "What kind of a man would I be if I went back on my word?"

"What kind of a woman would I be if I couldn't charm you into my apartment?"

"Well," he smiled, "if you put it that way."

Inside, he stopped in front of the fireplace, looking at Ethan's photographs. "How did he get interested in Afghanistan?"

"The only job he could get after he graduated that was

anywhere close to what he wanted was with CNN. They sent him to film the war. Which he hated. But he fell in love with the people and the country. He would sit and sleep on the floor, no chairs or beds. He always says he can feel the earth there. That it makes him feel as if he's part of something bigger."

She could repeat Ethan's words, but she was never exactly sure what he meant. More than once, he'd tried to explain. Over there, he said, his chest opens, and he feels peaceful—even in the middle of a war. He's *in* whatever he's doing, not watching it. But the only thing she'd ever been a part of was Ethan. She lifted her head and looked toward the door. The Fates. She was a part of them, too.

In the kitchen, she said, "Wine, beer, scotch?"

"What are you having?"

"Water and wine."

"You fix the water. I'll fix the wine. Have you ever been over there?"

She shook her head and looked back at the counter. Two wine glasses, two waters. Singer returning the wine to the fridge. If Setara could be in Ethan's bedroom, Singer could be in their apartment.

He nodded for her to go first, and she headed to the sofa, where she turned on the lamp. They passed drinks to each other as if this were high school. But nothing needed to be awkward. She'd known Singer longer even than she'd known Ethan. But they didn't know each other like this.

TV. She gave him the remote, her hand knocking against his strong one, her saying, "Ethan works the remote."

Singer found *My Cousin Vinny* in about two seconds. "How's this?" he said. "I've seen it so many times I can watch for as little as five minutes and enjoy it."

With the movie finally on, they could focus on something besides themselves. Each one spread out a little more, their shoulders touched, then their legs. This was how the end of the day was supposed to be. Except this wasn't her husband. She sat a little straighter.

Singer finished his wine and passed her the remote, but when their fingers touched again, this time, their eyes stuck. "I should go," he said, and he stood, collecting his empty wine glass and untouched water.

"Don't worry about the glasses," she said, but she didn't want him to leave.

At the door, he reached for the doorknob with one hand and rested the other on her arm, but she was pushing up the sleeves of her sweater so his hand landed on hers. He leaned down and kissed her on the cheek. "Thanks for the wine," he said. But his mouth grazed her hair and her fingers wrapped around his and there was less space between them rather than more. He held her close and tight and she was thinking if they could just hold on a minute, this thing that had hold of them would pass, his hand still on her hand on her sleeve. But his mouth found its way to hers and he really kissed her, and she kissed him back. And she could feel his hands through her thin spring sweater, moving from her arms to her hips when she thought, *This isn't high school. I'm married. I love Ethan.* She stepped back.

"I'm sorry," they said at the same time, each looking at the door.

"I got carried away," he said.

"It was my fault."

"Clearly not," he said, opening the door. "Really sorry, Cass." And then he was gone.

She shut the door and let her head fall against it. She had kissed someone not Ethan.

She raised her head, wondering what time it was.

Eleven fifteen. And no call. While she had been kissing Singer, Ethan had been not calling.

But she had learned not to panic—her mother had always panicked—only to make a mental note. He would call tomorrow.

She leaned against the door, staring at the empty apartment and missing Ethan with that sharp feeling she got at the airport when she'd just been holding onto him and then he was reaching for his bags. At that moment, she always seemed to be balancing on the curb, never standing square on the sidewalk. That moment— the changing from here into gone. One foot would fall to the street as she watched him step away from her, and she would turn to get into the car, telling herself not to look but she would, just in time to see the doors swallow his three bags and his broad shoulders.

20

After Singer left, Cass burrowed in, reaching to hit the light switch as she passed by the kitchen. The total darkness surprised her, as did having forgotten to turn on the light in the bedroom. Trailing her hand along the wall, she stopped at the threshold. The towel meant nothing—she could see that now. Across the dark room, lights from the city. Weeks ago, she had stood here watching Ethan stare out those windows into the dark. *Had* the towel meant nothing? It was all mixed up, and she didn't know what to think anymore.

She felt her way into the room, and in a few strides was fumbling with the switch to the lamp on her desk. She pulled back the quilt, kicked off her flip-flops, and in her clothes crawled in on her side. Once under the covers, instead of avoiding it, she looked at Ethan's side. By his night table, she couldn't tell if he were here or gone, the lamp and clock the only things ever there, his water glass always abandoned by the kitchen sink so he wouldn't crash into it in his sleep. The top of the dresser on the opposite wall held nothing but the oblong bowl where he dumped his change that she periodically collected and where he kept his passport-size wallet that was not there, which told her he was not in the apartment but not how far away he was. Even when he was gone, she slept only on her half of the bed. Sometimes, in the middle of the night, she pretended that instead of the smooth, empty surface behind her, he was where he was supposed to be, curled into a ball.

She turned over, facing her desk, and pressed her finger against her lips until they hurt. These were supposed to be the last days he'd be there—*forever*. But the air seemed uncertain. During the day, their wall of windows filled the room with light, but at night the giant darkness spilled into the room, accumulating in the corners first before pushing into the center until it was just her and the one tiny lamp on her desk.

In the kitchen of her childhood home at Randolph Air Force Base, there was only one tiny lamp. And next to it, a creepy long-necked pitcher with a swan's neck handle. Handblown glass with the tiny bubbles trapped forever, a heart painfully etched on the front, a cork in the top for good measure. In front of the lamp and the pitcher sat the bowl of fake lemons, and in front of the lemons was the spot her mother left her coffee mug and ashtray. When Cass got home from school, she would open all the windows and doors, flip on all the lights. But later, when her mother came home, she turned *off* all the lights except for the one where she was, as if she couldn't remember—or didn't want to—that Cass was there and might come out of her room. And when Cass did come out, she crept from lamp to lamp, island to island, until she could make it back to her desk.

This desk beside her—the one object in the house she had loved. It had been with her then and was here with her now. The top surface was flat. Books lined the back between elephant bookends, one narrow drawer in the middle, and in place of legs, four drawers on each side of the nook for the chair, a brass handle on the front of each of the drawers. Still lying on her side, she reached over and lifted one and let it fall.

Until Ethan's last trip, his being gone had never felt like stopping nor his return like starting again. He was simply here or there. But now she felt as if she were being jerked up and dropped. She was losing her ability to handle it. They were so close.

Again, she lifted a brass handle and let it fall. And then again. Three times, the sound of her father telling her goodnight.

When she was seven, maybe eight, on the base before Randolph, she decided not to live with her mother anymore and to go with her dad the next time he left. Her suitcase, the same floral tapestry one that was in her closet now, had been too big for her then, but she'd kept it open under her bed and filled it little by little. When it came time for her father to ship out on his next tour, she slid the suitcase out, zipped it up, and ran after him, right past her mother sitting in the den. Cass called to him, but he must not have heard, his camouflaged legs getting farther and farther away as she struggled over sidewalk cracks with her bag. Her arms had ached, but she'd kept struggling until he disappeared, and then she sat on the curb, waiting for him to come get her. At dusk, she started back home. When she opened the front door, her mother was still in the den, but sitting in the dark, smoking a cigarette. And Cass had drifted, from lamp to lamp, through the dark, empty house, dragging her suitcase behind her.

21

Through the peephole, Katie was holding a mass of pink in her arms. Cass opened the door. "Oh, dear. You didn't bring your key back the last time."

"I'm not locked out," Katie said. "Is Ethan here?"

"He'll be back on Friday."

"Well, I know you're not much of a baby person, but..." And then without asking, Katie dumped the pink mass into Cass's stiff arms. "Apparently, my mother has broken her ankle. Thank heavens she did it on Saturday."

"I can't," Cass said, the extra weight drawing her down but causing her to straighten up at the same time.

Katie dropped a pink bag, carry-on size, at Cass's planted feet. "You know I can't take a baby to the germy ER."

Cass didn't know that.

"Tom was on his way out of town," Katie said, heading down the hall, "but he's turned around. He should be here in an hour."

"I can't take care of a baby."

"Sure, you can." Katie picked up speed. "I owe you," she yelled, punching the elevator button and disappearing.

"I can't," Cass said again, standing in the hall staring at the line of closed doors.

She couldn't take care of a baby. She had a baby in her arms. A baby.

Shutting the door with her back, she leaned against it, her pulse accelerating. She felt it move. Glancing down, she saw closed eyes, a nose, a mouth. It was so little. She wondered if she could put the baby on the sofa, but as she propped the bundle in the corner, she knew that was a bad idea. If she just put it on the floor, it couldn't fall.

She would put it under the coffee table. That way, nothing could fall *on* it.

Cass kneeled and felt dizzy. She exhaled and reached under the table to deposit the baby but was struck by a feeling of déjà vu. It moved again. And cried, but it seemed almost like fake crying. The little thing wiggled and stretched her arms, too. The blanket got on her face, and Cass reached under the table to remove it.

Cass sat on the sofa and put the bag in her lap. Maybe she could find directions. But maybe she should sit on the floor where she could see the baby. She uncovered her face again. Apparently, she did need to watch her all the time.

In the bag, a stack of Winnie the Pooh diapers that horrified her. And there were creams in tubes, wipes, a blanket, clothes, several cans of formula, an empty bottle, a pacifier. Where were the instructions?

Louder crying.

Cass found an outside pocket, and when she reached in, paper. But it was just telephone numbers. On the other side, nothing.

She stared at the baby, the helpless baby, the child dependent on the grown-ups around her. But there was no one around except Cass.

Kneeling again, she reached forward, gripping the blanket and sliding the screaming baby out. Tears speckled her tiny face, and Cass wasn't quite sure how to pick her up—how had Katie handed her over. The best she could figure was to scoop her up like a stack of logs for the fireplace. Working not to lose her balance, she managed to stand, and then she walked. And sang. *Silent Night,* the only quiet song she could think of.

Like some sort of miracle, they both calmed down. But as Cass crossed into the bedroom on the third turn around the apartment, she almost bumped the baby's head against the doorframe. Her heart squeezed tight, and she stopped. The baby cried. Cass cupped her hand around the little head and began to move again. *All is calm. All is bright.*

○ ○ ○

After the baby was gone, their apartment retook its familiar shape. Her desk became her desk again.

How could she ever be a mother? It had taken everything she had to keep the baby alive for an hour. She dropped into her chair. One hour, though. She had kept it alive for an hour. But she hadn't been able to think about anything except survival—hers and the baby's.

Cass leaned forward, onto her elbows. There was something else she couldn't quite identify. She tapped her fingernails on the wood—faster and faster until she couldn't make her fingers go any faster and she balled her hand into a fist.

If she had a baby, Ethan would not be Ethan anymore; instead, he would be somebody's father, somebody she was waiting for who could take care of the baby so she could think about something else. And then *Ethan* would have the baby. Being two together— what she had been waiting for her whole life—would be over. If she had a baby, it would never be just the two of them again.

○ ○ ○

When he called at eleven, the phone rang only once.

22

As Cass approached Howell House, so much was bothering her that she couldn't isolate anything. Fingers on latte, eyes on ground. Focus. She was almost at the front door before she noticed Lois sitting outside.

"Hey there," Cass said, heading toward the old trees and the raised area that was grassy and shady. Two wrought iron chairs sat on either side of a small table.

"I didn't see you coming," Lois said.

"Seems like we were both somewhere else," Cass said, sitting down and putting her latte on the table, where there were four piles of three acorns each.

"I woke up thinking of my mother," Lois said, sitting straight, her shoes not reaching the grass, a red beret on her strange yellow hair, her mother-of-pearl glasses on her nose, and red lipstick on her mouth. "She sat outside every morning. If it was raining, she sat on the front stoop. After a night of sleep, she said she needed to reconnect with the world."

Cass's fingers curled up as she remembered tugging on her mother's hair, her mother's dresses, her mother's shoes. As she remembered the hair, the dresses, and the shoes yanked away.

"Do you see your mother often?" Lois asked.

Cass shook her head. "She killed herself the day after I left for college."

"Oh, that is so sad. She couldn't live without you."

"It wasn't because she would miss me. It was for the life she had missed. The last thing I heard my mother say was to my father. 'I was supposed to have a life,' she said. 'Instead I had a child, and now I don't even have that.' "

"Ah," Lois said. "*My* mother led me out here this morning so you could talk about *your* mother. She was like that." Lois reached her hand across the table, and Cass took it.

But what Cass heard was her mother's crackly smoker's voice—the voice that made Cass feel small—*I gave up everything for you.* Another of her mother's refrains.

"The birds," Lois said. "Listen to the birds."

○ ○ ○

Later, Cass went by the library to meet up with Vee for an after-work beer. It had been almost two weeks since the kiss, and she'd put Vee off as long as she could. Working late on fundraising had been her excuse as well as the truth. But she missed Vee and thought she could handle seeing Singer again.

As Vee bounced from wall to wall, turning out lights, Cass took a step backward, into the stillness of the stacks, and ran her fingers along the books. So much happens between the covers of these books. So much happens under the surface. Which made Cass think of May's fortune about things being done on her behalf.

"Just the alarm," Vee said. "And we'll be free."

Outside, the air was a different still. As if time had stopped, as if nothing was happening or would ever happen again.

"So, how's Dillon?" Cass asked, as they turned off Howell Mill into the development.

"How's Ethan?"

"He really doesn't care when you get home?"

"Why is that so hard to believe?"

"When Ethan's here—only three more days, by the way—I go straight home after work. He does the same."

"Maybe I don't want to see him."

"Is that it?"

"It would be so much better if we could choose from objective criteria. For example, one who didn't drink."

"For example, one who didn't work in Afghanistan."

"We both knew what we were choosing," Vee said. "Yet we did it anyway."

But she and Ethan had fixed that. With the agreement.

"I messed up, Vee."

"You messed up?"

"Singer kissed me, and I kissed him back."

Vee stopped and leaned against a tree. "Okay," she said. "That's okay. It was just a kiss." She waved her hand in the air. "Right?"

Cass nodded, but when it came to her and Ethan, kissing someone else could never be *just a kiss*. It wasn't a small thing—it was terrible.

"Forget it. We all make mistakes. I'm sure Ethan does, too."

Cass jerked her head up.

"Not that kind of mistake," Vee said. "Other mistakes."

They were moving again, toward the bar.

"Also, I babysat over the weekend."

"You babysat?"

"Katie, my neighbor, her mother broke her ankle, and apparently it's not good to take a baby to the ER. I guess there was no one else. The baby was in my arms and Katie was gone before I knew what had happened. I didn't want to do it, but it's good I did. Not sure why I hadn't done it before. But it's done now."

"What's done?"

"Holding a baby."

"You'd never held a baby before?"

"Can we stop for a second?" She took Vee's arm and drew her out of the walkway. She could hear the music from the bar, muted but in the air. "I need to tell you something else."

They stood in the midst of the picnic tables across from the bar. Vee leaned against one and placed her purse to the side.

Cass intertwined her fingers. "You know I've been trying to

want kids, but when I held that baby, I just didn't feel anything. Except anxious. But, I mean, no desire for one of my own. Nothing." She looked away. "I don't want kids. I just can't."

"Nobody's making you have kids."

"Ethan might," Cass said, and she stopped again.

"But it's just you and me right now."

"I mean he said it was okay if I didn't. A long time ago. And he's not a bully. Jeez. It's just—"

"He's been counting on you to change your mind."

Cass nodded. "I think so."

"Listen," Vee said, as they continued on, "you've done what Ethan asked you to. You even babysat. But something is telling you children are not for you. You know something about yourself. Good for you, I say."

"I hate this for Ethan. I just hate it. He wants to be a father. His died before he was born."

"If only he could be a father without you being a mother," Vee said.

"That wouldn't help." Cass felt her face heat up. "The two of us—that's what I've been waiting for." She stamped her foot. "I'm the most selfish person on the planet."

"It's good to know what you need." Vee cleared her throat. "Sometimes you just have to stand up for yourself."

Cass opened the door for Vee but hung back a minute before going in. Ethan was on a different continent, where they spoke a different language, asleep when she was awake. Cass shut her eyes, and when she did, the wind swirled around her as if someone were wrapping her in a cocoon, taking care of her. And the sensation felt so familiar, but she couldn't place it. She had always loved the wind. She never felt all the way alone in its presence.

○ ○ ○

Inside, Singer was making his way toward Vee. "How are you?" he asked. Then Cass sat down, and nobody said anything. She looked around as if Singer weren't there, which was ridiculous, but she couldn't look *at* him.

"Okay you two," Vee said, "am I supposed to pretend I don't know?"

"Vee," Cass said.

"For fuck's sake," Vee said. "We're all friends. Shake hands and agree to play nice from now on."

Singer smiled and reached his hand across the wooden counter, and Cass took it, feeling not Singer's hand but Ethan's callused one the night they met, how he'd kept holding her hand, how she'd thought he'd never give it back.

23

Amidst a crowd of people at the Atlanta airport, Cass stood waiting for Ethan. On her tiptoes, she thought she saw him—dark hair rising on the escalator. It *was* him. But with a beard. He was crossing the arrivals lobby, then kissing her, the rough hairs interfering, the foreign smell of cigarettes around the collar of his shirt.

"Are you okay?"

"I'm exhausted."

His eyes were glassy and bloodshot, swollen underneath, brushing over her but not sticking, as if the surface of her were no longer anywhere they could rest. He kept one hand on her, but it kept moving—waist, back, shoulder, arm, hand—as they proceeded to baggage claim and to the parking lot. Before they crossed the street, he glanced in her direction but not at her.

It was so disorienting to see him with a beard that she half expected him to take it off, as if it were fake and hooked over his ears like glasses. And like a child she wanted him to take it off. But hair also grew above his mouth and from his mouth down to his chin, a small patch of endangered skin on each side.

"I thought shaving helped you make the transition," she said, as she gave him her keys. She thought it helped him remember where he was.

"There were lines for the bathroom," he said, heaving his bags into the back of her Explorer. "Does it matter?" he asked.

She reached her hand up to one side of his face, her thumb on his cheek, her fingers in his beard. "Of course not," she said.

He covered her hand with his, turned it to him and inhaled, closing his eyes.

But her Ethan didn't have a beard.

○ ○ ○

After she opened her car door in their damp parking garage, she reached to open the back. "Leave the bags," he said, grabbing her hand. He beeped the car locked behind them.

In the car, they'd barely spoken. As if he were only just holding himself together, as if he were trying to make it *until*, but until what she didn't know.

They waited a few seconds for the elevator, but then, without a word, he pulled her behind him to the stairs, up to street level, up three flights, and into their apartment. He threw the door shut. She was out of breath.

No talking, no velvet touches, no shower first. He pushed her up against the door, kissing her with a hunger that at first made her wonder where the need came from but within seconds there were no more thoughts, only their hands, their mouths, their bodies. A dark propulsion that past a certain point surprised her with its familiarity, as if she, too, contained it within her.

He never looked at her. It was not about sight but feel. Body to body. Dropping to the cold, wood floor. No bed. Nothing soft.

He kept going; she wasn't sure how—he in that condition of exhaustion where she positioned her body between herself and the world, where she kept everything closed, separate, shielded, and yet, here he opened up. Her head against the wood, his hands in her hair, his kisses landing on her forehead, the wings of her nose, behind her ears, down her neck, to the rounded curve of her shoulder.

And only here, in the hollow of her clavicle, did he find her. And when he did, he held on so tight she couldn't breathe. She had always been his safe place. But in the minutes since he'd arrived, it was only now that she felt he knew he was home. When it was over, he was instantly, and deeply, asleep.

They lay on the floor at right angles—her body face up; his, facedown. They overlapped in one spot—his mouth, her shoulder. She scooted out from under him, cradling his head as she reached for his shirt to soften the wood floor. Then she sat up. Their clothes lay in a pile, dropped all at once, no trail. She leaned back against the blue wheelbarrow and pulled her knees to her chest. As if in response, he pulled his body into the ball she recognized, his back inches from where she sat. Her skin stung, his beard having scraped bits of her away, bits that were ready to go, bits that obscured. His back—she could still feel its heat. At his waist, the jagged, boomerang-shaped scar. That phone call his first trip after the wedding. He'd said it was nothing. Running to a safe house, a bullet hit him and he'd fallen at the searing pain and heat of it, woken in the hospital. It was the only bad thing that had ever happened. Her fingers always went there during sex, the uneven skin over the wound a place to hold onto, a way in.

Maybe if she had a scar.

She stood, and he shifted—out of the ball and into a straight line, onto his stomach. She covered him with a throw and headed to the shower. Usually, they showered together, fell asleep entangled, and woke at the same time. Her stomach rumbled. She couldn't remember a trip since she'd known him that he hadn't shaved before he arrived home.

$$\circ \, ^\circ \, \circ$$

When she woke beside him on the floor, the room was veiled in darkness. Out the windows, black clouds. The time, a little before noon. He was snoring. She scooted closer and closed her eyes again.

He began to turn from side to side. She touched his arm, and he jumped.

"What?" he said, sitting up fast.

"You were tossing."

He stood and took small, pinched steps toward the hall. "My legs are cramping."

She sat up. "I'm hungry. You?"

"Shower."

She watched him limp away before standing and restoring order. In the kitchen, she took out juice, eggs and bacon, raspberry jam. She pulled bread from the bread drawer; if only she could pull what she needed to say from inside herself and leave it next to the bread. But this wasn't the right time—the first three days belonged to them—the two of them—not to talk of children.

When he came in a few minutes later, she was turning the bacon.

"I don't think I want breakfast," he said. "What about a BLT? Do we have lettuce and tomato?"

She looked at him, standing there in the middle of the kitchen—wet hair and clean and handsome, even with the beard.

"Usually," she said, planning to say more.

"I know," he said. "Usually, we have breakfast. I'm just hungry for something else."

He came toward her. It was possible the beard made him more handsome.

"We could add a fried egg?" he said.

24

Three a.m. Straight up. Her hand reached to the other side of the bed. No Ethan.

Closing her eyes, she drew her arm underneath her. A black-and-white movie, spotty, the reel clicking. Shuffling home after school. Bending to pick up the newspaper covered in rubber bands. Emptying her mother's ashtray. Cass opened her eyes and sat up. She stood, trying to get her bearings. Someone was smoking. But in the hall, no lights. And no one in the kitchen. As she crossed into the den, she saw a figure standing on the balcony, the tiny orange glow of a cigarette, smoke dissolving into the air.

She crept closer and heard his voice, low. And first her legs froze, then the hairs on her arms, and then, one by one, the vessels of her heart. It didn't make sense. Nothing made sense.

Turning to go back to her room, she woke enough to wonder why she wasn't going forward, why she hadn't spoken. She stopped in the dark hall, placed two fingers on her heart and pressed down, as if to stop the bleeding. Standing still, listening to Ethan's voice—"well, I'll just...if I have to...assume nothing is safe"—she felt dizzy. When she reached to steady herself, the door of the guest bathroom gave way, and she was jarred into righting herself.

Again she turned, but this time she went forward, into the den.

He was facing her—he must have heard the door. His index finger punched off the phone, and, as if he did it all the time, he tossed the cigarette over his shoulder into the night. He stepped into the room. But she held up her hand and forced herself past him onto the balcony to lean against the railing into the wide expanse of darkness. She breathed in the air, laced with her mother's sadness.

Ethan felt too close, but that was the only way for both of them to be here. Too close. She could never have imagined such a thing.

His first words. "It was Setara."

Of course, it was.

"But it's not what you think."

She focused on the strongest, brightest star, and said, "How could you possibly know what I'm thinking?"

He didn't try to touch her, and she was unsure if that was to his credit.

"You smoke now, too?"

"Not *now*," he said. "Over there. Sometimes."

Brick floor, iron railing, a breeze so slight she almost missed it.

"It's noon in Kabul," he said. "Our investors—"

"By *our*, you mean?"

"Setara's and mine."

She would make him say it from now on.

"CNN, in particular, has put a lot of money into this project of teaching the Afghans how to take photos. Now we—"

"Who?"

"Now Setara and I have to figure out how to proceed because there's been some interference. One death."

"Somebody was killed?"

"One of Setara's runners, a messenger, was hit by a government car."

"Jeez, Ethan."

"I know. It's unclear if it was intentional, if it was a warning. That's why we had to talk."

He turned around and leaned back against the railing, looking toward the roof of their building. "I knew I shouldn't have left when I did."

"Well, I'm glad you're here, and safe."

He turned and put his arm around her, and they stood together looking out into the darkness.

Surely there wasn't time for him to go back before their

anniversary, but she knew that there was. Still, he was here now, and she felt the strength in his arm holding her next to him, and she leaned against him and focused on the small twinkling lights of the city.

25

The first time Ethan traveled to Afghanistan after they started dating, Cass had googled her.

Setara Keshwar Kamal is the subject of a photographic portrait made by the American photographer Ethan Graham that was chosen for the cover of TIME magazine. Her beauty came to stand for the beauty of Afghanistan and for beauty everywhere in the war-torn world.

Setara Kamal is the youngest of four children. Her sister was the oldest, married at fifteen to a man who beat her when her first child was a girl and beat her to death when her second child was also a girl. Then he suffocated each child. At the age of twelve, after a bomb destroyed her home, killing the rest of her family, Setara was sold by her uncle to a Pakistani man who pushed her over the border in a wheelbarrow. A British diplomat, visiting their refugee camp, bought her from the Pakistani and took her to England where he gave her his name and raised her as his daughter. When he died, Setara Bell returned to Afghanistan as a teacher. Shortly after her return, she married Feda Ali and joined the Revolutionary Association of the Women of Afghanistan (RAWA). Currently, Setara Ali works in partnership with her husband and Ethan Graham, whose photograph of her as The Afghan Woman *is known throughout the world.*

There was a link to a YouTube video.

And there he was. Ethan—younger, beautiful himself, an Ethan before she knew him. Thinner and lit by wonder. Sitting and talking to a reporter.

I was in Kabul with my fixer Baquir. We were headed down a hallway...on our way out of a university. Sunlight from a high window fell on a group of teachers wearing these amazing, colorful scarves. It's not easy to get photos of women, and Baquir was already retrieving my camera when I turned for it. I was cautious. Some of the teachers moved off to the side. But there was one woman in the back, next to a faded black wall, who did not turn toward me and yet seemed to be drawing me toward her. Shot after shot, in every photo, only her silvery gray back frosted in midnight blue. Setara would have stood out anyway, but by not facing me from the beginning, it became a kind of hunt, I guess. So I inched my way in, getting closer and closer to the wall, still shooting. When there was nothing in my lens other than her dark blue shayla, she turned, and there were those starlight amber eyes. Her scarf even then only a nod at covering her obsidian black hair. There was such power in that. Her eyebrows, only a frame for those eyes. I have to say, my camera fell away from my face.

Cass never googled Setara again. She was always there between them anyway—no need to go searching for her.

26

Day four. Cass was in her office when she heard the front door open. She waited to hear someone's voice, and then there was Ethan.

"Hey, there," he said.

She smiled and stood. It had been ages since he'd stopped by unannounced. "This is a nice surprise."

"I thought maybe I could take you to dinner," he said.

"Well, if it isn't the handsome husband?"

"Atta," he said, giving her a hug. "It's always great to see you."

"I think if you came by every day, we would all live longer. We would definitely live happier."

"Atta, you spoil me."

"Let me introduce you to Lois," Cass said, heading past Ethan and Atta toward the hallway.

"We're all in the breakfast room," Atta said, "trying to get Fanny to hurry supper up."

In the warm kitchen, which smelled of garlic and ground beef, Ethan said, "Hello, Fanny, I've come to interrupt your cooking."

"Oh, Mr. Ethan, you're a sight for sore eyes," she said, drying her hands on her apron.

"How many times have I asked you not to call me 'mister'?" he said, giving her a hug, too.

"Will you be eating with us? You love my lasagna. Cass always has me fix extra in case someone stops by."

"I'll take a rain check, Fanny. I'm hoping to take my wife out to dinner." He looked over at Cass.

"I think that's a fine idea," Fanny said. "The others are in there...waiting on me." She grinned and opened the oven.

After the introductions and hugs, Ethan sat down, so Cass

did, too. Fanny pushed open the swinging door to say five more minutes.

"Will you come do another slideshow?" Atta asked. "Now that Lois is here. I know she'd love to see your photos. And May and I always enjoy it."

"Oh, yes," Lois said. May nodded.

"That's a great idea," Cass said.

"I'd be proud to."

"Any new photos?" May asked.

"I'll have one on the cover of *TIME* next week. But it's an old photo."

"We like old things around here," Lois said, grinning at Atta.

○ ○ ○

Back in her office, Ethan whispered, "Lois's hair really is yellow. You weren't kidding."

"I told you," Cass said. "Just let me put things away. And make sure I'm set for tomorrow."

"This is a wonderful place," he said, sitting down. "You've done such a good job."

Cass smiled. She had nothing the next day until noon. She closed her computer and returned files to the drawer.

"I may have to go back, Cass."

Her hands fell to the desk.

"When I realized it an hour ago, after talking to Setara, I wanted to see you. I wasn't going to say anything because it's not for sure. But I just wanted to see you."

She stood and looked away from him, over the deck to the back yard.

"You and I," he said and then paused.

She sat back down, waiting.

He leaned forward. "Can we try to stay on the same side?"

This was the time to say what she had to say. But he couldn't go back now. "It's not just that I don't want you to leave again. It's more dangerous now. Somebody was killed over there, Ethan. Having to do with *your* project."

"Maybe," he said, sitting back in the chair. "Probably." He looked toward the foyer. "Before I left Kabul, I held Setara's baby. You know, growing up, it was always just my mother and me. Only the two of us. I never got to have the feeling you have here of being surrounded by family. Two always felt like something was missing."

Was it possible they'd each been holding a baby at the same time? Her arms wrapped around her stomach. "I've told you about seeing that little girl lying on the pavement, and the little black dog, about her mother seeing it all, too."

"I know, babe," he said. "In Afghanistan...well, I get how seeing something like that can tear you up."

And then she got why she was avoiding telling him what she'd already told Vee. Because then her part of Tidal Flats would be over, and Ethan would know there was no hope.

He leaned forward again. "But, look, what I also want to say is if I don't have you, none of the rest matters. Even if that means no children. But I can't help what I want. And what I want is a child with you."

And for the first time, she thought, *Don't give me what I want. I don't want to win.*

How had this become about winning and losing?

"This is personal, Ethan. Howell isn't the place to talk about it."

He stood and came around her desk and pulled her from the chair. He squeezed her as if he would never go anywhere without her. "This *is* the place to talk about it. That's why Howell is amazing." He kissed her and said, "Let's go eat. Let's go have some fun."

27

The next day after work, although Cass didn't often go when Ethan was home, she went to the bar. She just needed a little breath of something that wasn't Ethan or Howell.

As Singer leaned on the counter in front of her, his smile and warmth seemed too easy. "Long time, no see," he said, giving her his full attention. Vee wasn't there yet.

"Ethan's home," she said, wishing for the early days of being married when nothing but music accompanied those words.

"Ah," he said, straightening up, placing a blank coaster in front of her. "The usual?" he asked.

"Yes," she said, thankful. When he delivered her beer, she thought she was going to say something else. Her lips parted. He waited.

At that moment, Vee plopped down beside her. "Heaven."

Singer smiled at Vee. "Be right back."

"Is it all candlelight and kisses having the hubby home?" Vee twirled in her seat, to the left and to the right, but not all the way around, which is what Cass expected.

"Is it all candlelight and kisses with Dillon?" Cass said, looking at her and raising her eyebrows.

"Point taken," she said and stopped twirling.

Singer set Vee's beer in front of her and disappeared. Two bartenders tonight, both busy.

"Being married is hard," Cass said.

"From my personal experience," Vee said, "the problem appears to be that it involves two people."

"Precisely," Cass said. "He's desperate for a child."

"You told him."

"I did not." Cass took another gulp of beer, setting her glass down in exactly the same spot on the coaster. "I don't know how."

"Talk to me," Vee said.

Cass felt as if she'd fallen out of an inner tube and was watching the current take it farther and farther away, and at the same time she also felt as if she were *in* the inner tube drifting farther and farther away.

"When Ethan gets over there," Cass said, "he wears their clothes. Doesn't shave. Stays in their houses. Smokes apparently. He becomes an Afghan."

"Well, he needs to, right? To blend in. It's safer that way."

"Here," Cass said, "he wears American clothes. Stays in our apartment. Shaves." She looked at Vee. "But he came home this time with a beard."

"Maybe he got confused."

Cass picked up her beer.

Vee picked up hers, the birds, or bird, of her tattoo flying up her forearm toward the beer and freedom.

"So how are things with Dillon?" Cass said.

Vee looked away.

"See, sometimes, it's not so much fun to talk."

"It's better to talk," Vee said.

"So don't you like him at all?"

"Dillon..." she said, and hesitated, and Cass wasn't sure she'd ever seen her hesitate. "Dillon and I are separated."

"Oh, Vee."

"I'm not married, not divorced. I'm in the middle of failing."

"I'm so sorry."

"I'm sorry for me, too."

"I'm a bad friend."

"No, I deliberately hid this. I wasn't ready. It was those weeks I disappeared. When Ethan was home before. I talk a big game, but I don't know how to talk about this. I'm sorry I didn't tell you sooner."

"No need to be sorry," she said. "I get it."

Singer came by. "Cheer up, girls. Nothing an order of truffle fries won't fix, right?"

"I'd take some truffle fries," Vee said, looking at her.

Cass glanced at her watch. Ethan would be home now, but she'd left a note telling him she was getting a beer and then would be back. "I have time to eat a few of yours," she said.

Singer scooted away. Cass said, "What can I do to help?"

"You're doing it."

"Do the two of you have a plan?"

"I love him, but I can't live with him. I can't see over that."

Monday night's crowd was sparse so far, and the space felt good. "Do you know what you want?"

"I don't actually." Vee set her beer down and a little sloshed out. "You know, I like things that spill over. Messes make me comfortable. They take the pressure off."

Singer delivered the fries.

"Exactly what we need," Vee said.

Cass looked from the fries to Singer.

"Break bread with us," Vee said to Singer.

"I was hoping you'd say that." And he picked up a fry that was leaning in his direction. He filled Cass's glass with water. "Good thing I have backup tonight. Five-minute break for my favorite thing on the menu and my favorite people on the stools."

"You can always count on the truffle fries," Cass said.

Singer put his hand on Cass's arm. "Yes, you can."

"I feel better already," Cass said.

And then Singer looked up. He smiled and lifted his hand off Cass's arm. When she turned, Ethan was standing behind her.

"Hey," she said.

In Ethan's pause before he stepped forward, she was afraid that as a couple, they were too unsure of where each one stood in relation to the other to be out in the world.

Ethan shook hands with Singer. "It's been a while," Ethan said. "How's it going?" Singer said.

Ethan turned to Vee and smiled, bending down to kiss her cheek. "How are you?"

"It's been too long," Vee said.

He took a step closer to Cass and gave her a squeeze. Maybe adding other people into the mix was exactly what they needed.

"Only a minute ago," Singer said, "Cass was saying you'd just gotten home. I can't imagine all that travel. I guess I'm just a homebody."

"Tell me about Dubai," Vee said. "That's a place I'd like to go just because of its name. Sometimes I can be really superficial."

"Unfortunately," he said. "I only know the airport."

"You want to sit down and get a beer?" Cass asked.

"On the house," Singer said.

"I thought I might want a beer," Ethan said, "but I think I'd rather go on back. Jet lag, I guess."

"You go ahead," she said, touching his hand and then wrapping hers around her glass.

Singer excused himself to get back to work. "Great to see you, Ethan."

"You too, Singer." Ethan turned to her. "You're not ready?"

"I'm going to stay a little longer," she said, even though she could tell he needed her, needed her to claim him, and she didn't understand why she didn't.

"See you at home then." He touched her shoulder. "Bye, Vee."

Cass lifted a French fry to her mouth, the solidified grease weighing it down. She had about a third of her beer left, but the fizz and sharpness had gone out of it, and it wasn't cold anymore.

"It's like in between seeing him," Vee said. "I forget how cute he is."

Singer went by with drinks. "Can I get you anything else, Cass?"

"Another beer. Definitely."

"What am I, chopped liver?" Vee said.

"You were next," he said, pausing. "So, you want another beer?"

"What do you think?" Vee said.

"That's why I love you," Singer said, as he continued on.

Cass said, "Singer's so nice."

"Singer *is* nice. But he's not Ethan. And if you ask me, which you didn't, I think you need to tell Ethan where you are with the kid thing. Avoiding him is not going to help. He knew no kids was a risk. My bet is he'll handle it. I just don't think you can take the photos he takes without being a good guy."

$$\circ \,{}^{\circ}\, \circ$$

When Cass got home thirty minutes later, all the lights were off in the apartment. She started to call out but instead tiptoed down the hall, stopping at the threshold of their room, where she could just make out Ethan's shape under the covers. Maybe he really was jet-lagged. She pulled the door closed and slipped off her shoes.

In the kitchen, she turned on the light. She was keyed up and needed to do something before she opened her book. She lowered the door to the dishwasher and turned on the water and was rinsing the last plate when Ethan's arms circled her waist and she smelled verbena—the new soap she'd bought.

She let go of the plate.

He reached around her and shut off the water. Then he stood in front of her.

"I need to tell you something," she said.

"Let's don't talk right now," he said, and he reached his rough hands to her face. He kissed her mouth and her ears and her neck. She could feel his fingers through her white cotton shirt, through her camisole and thin bra, on the sides of her breasts. He untucked her camisole and his hands attached to her skin in the way she loved, so she could feel every surface of every finger, then his fingers slid down under the belt of her jeans, under the edge of her underwear. She threaded her fingers through his thick hair that curled on his neck. Their arms crossed over each other's as they unbuttoned shirts. He peeled hers off her shoulders, down her arms, and lifted the camisole up over her head and without a pause, he picked her up and carried her to their bed where she pulled his face to hers and kissed him. And he began again, kissing her ears, her neck, and winding his way down, his fingers catching her bra straps in their wake. But he stopped and looked into her eyes, and she knew, just as she had known that day at the breakwater, that he wanted to be here with her and nowhere else in the world.

28

May was sitting in her favorite chair in her bedroom but looking in at the room instead of out the window as she usually did.

"Cass, is that you?"

May was looking straight at her.

"It's me. Ella said you were having trouble seeing this morning."

"Only with my eyes," May said and giggled.

"I'll call the doctor."

"No need," May said. "He told me this would happen. Now it has."

"I want to be you when I grow up."

"You're going to be so much more than me, Cass. That warms my heart."

Several books lay open facedown on the other chair. Cass moved them to the floor. Despite the fact that May couldn't read anymore, she liked to open her books, smell them, smooth her hands over the words, and down the pages. On the small round table between them, three lavender roses in a crystal vase and a tin of rose balm.

"Howell wasn't supposed to run out of money," Cass said. "That wasn't part of my plan."

"Plans are good," May said, "but life is the thing. Living. And dancing even when the music changes. Where would we be if our plans just unrolled before us?"

"Is that you or the Madame speaking?"

"It's all of us."

Cass looked closer at May and then at the piles around the room—other books, sweaters, tote bags, papered boxes with lids.

"It's just the center that's blurry. I can still see around the edges. Before you came in, I was thinking about a little hummingbird I once knew. I haven't thought of her in ages. I was almost sixty. Ha, over thirty years ago now. I was in the kitchen drinking coffee and reading. I had opened the window all the way. My hair was long then, and thick like a broomstick. The wind was blowing strands into my mouth. The pages of the book were ruffling. And there was the hummingbird, just outside the window."

May looked toward the window. Cass did too.

"The next thing I knew the tiny bird had darted inside and into my hair. I could feel her on my head—a heaviness and a lightness at the same time, her constant motion stilled. Harvey was the only other person in the house and sequestered in his office working. Anyway, I didn't want a man to wrench a delicate hummingbird out of my hair. It didn't seem right. I inched to the mirror by the front door—so carefully, as if I were balancing a book on my head. She was a beautiful bird, proud gray silk wings, a pink throat. As I was standing in front of the mirror, Harvey came up behind me. 'Ah,' he said, 'the hummingbird's blessing of joy.' And he did a little bow."

May paused and smiled. Sometimes Cass just wanted to stay in this room with May forever.

"Harvey took off his shirt—he was a good-looking man—and so gently, with such feeling in his hands, and with such respect for this tiny, wild creature, he scooped that bird into his shirt and released her outside. I had wanted to do it myself, but it seemed as if the task were meant for him, as if we were caught in the service of something bigger. Almost as if that little bird had called him into the foyer so I could see that inside this man there were wondrous things I had yet to discover."

29

When Cass started out for Howell the next morning, it was too bright, too shiny. Like the hot summers at her grandparents' house in Mobile, where after the brightness usually came the shattering, and then the running, often down the short hall away from the mirror at its end, away from her mother's unhappiness with something Cass had done. She crossed Howell Mill, anxious that was where this day was headed. And it wasn't even summer yet.

The day her mother threw a hairbrush breaking that mirror, Cass was so little she'd had to use both hands to turn the knob on the back door. Four giant white steps and then full speed for the sweet smell of the roses. Under the clothesline and through the metal gate, into her secret garden, sticking her nose into an orange bloom.

"That's a Tropicana," Paw Paw had said, putting his arm around her. "Just laying eyes on it always makes me feel better. Kind of fruity, don't you think?"

Cass looked up into the light, as her body continued to heave.

"There's a pretty pink one I want to show you over here."

She loved how he kept the colors separate. It seemed to make the flowers stronger somehow.

"This is the Landmark Rose," he said. "It was your mother's favorite when she was your age."

"It's beautiful," Cass said, even though she didn't want it to be. White ruffled edges. Pink in the middle.

"Smell it," he said.

She sniffed. "It's sweet. I remember the smell. Almost too sweet."

"But it's nice, isn't it?"

"Can we see the white ones, the ones that grow on the fence?" Those were Cass's favorites.

He stood. "Do you remember their name?"

"White something," she said. "About the morning. White Dawn."

"Yes," he said, smiling. "And White Dawn climbs up, no matter where I plant her." He squatted down beside her. "Honey, your mother does the best she can. There's nothing wrong with you. You're just what a little girl is supposed to be."

As Cass opened the door to Howell, she wondered what her grandfather would say to her now.

30

Comfort food. Ever since Ethan had come up the escalator with the beard, Cass had needed comforting. It was true he was home, but it was as if they were stuck on a roller coaster, unable to find a minute of solid ground.

Standing at the sink in front of the window, she peeled potatoes and tossed them into boiling water. In her largest metal bowl, she smashed the too-red curls of ground beef together with the oatmeal and Worcestershire sauce and ketchup. When a tendril of beef tried to escape between her fingers, she caught it and pushed it back into the whole, forcing them all into one, single meat loaf. When the potatoes were done, she discarded the water and mashed until there was no sign of what each had once been. The green beans. Finally, something that refused to compromise.

She wanted what she wanted, not something else, something watered down, something that wasn't. She had prided herself on her independence. She had needed no one. Safe in her apartment in Virginia Highlands, she had needed no one until she met Ethan.

○ ○ ○

He came home around six but worked in the den. When she went in to ask what time he'd like to eat, three rows of three photographs each were lined up on the coffee table. The top six were square, each of a man's face. The bottom three were rectangles, each of two boys.

He stood, a package in his hand.

"I forgot to give this to you," he said, holding it out to her.

A packet that fit in her palm, a stiff blue paper case holding five or six sheets of cream-colored homemade paper, each sheet with a deckled edge. Like us, she thought. And she looked into his blue eyes. "It's lovely," she said.

She liked to imagine that he happened upon these things and thought of her, that he saw her in the world around him, wherever he was, not that he went searching for something to bring her. It wasn't every trip but most trips. Ethan's father had taken his mother small gifts, too. One of these, a cream-colored comb with a gold filigree along the edge, she had loaned Cass to wear in her hair for their wedding.

$$\circ \, ^\circ \, \circ$$

By the time they got to the table, Cass felt as if she were straining to reach something while trying to avoid falling off a ladder, although she knew that in order to reach what she needed, she would have to propel her feet off the firm, narrow surface on which she stood.

After dinner, she offered to do the dishes, but eventually, she ran out of tasks and went to join him on the sofa. The boys were still on the coffee table, and in each of the photographs, she noticed now, there was something that needed protecting and something that needed changing. In the one of the two sitting on a roadside boulder sharing a book, each small boy was wide-eyed, but the shell of a car burned beside them, orange flames against a bright blue sky.

Cass felt wound up, as if all she needed was to let go and the rest would take care of itself. She cleared her throat. "I need to tell you something." She had told him something before—years ago at Stone Mountain. She could do it again.

He looked at her.

"I never wanted children," she said. It was true, and it was where she had to start. "Maybe it came through the air from my mother not wanting me, or maybe it came from her attempts to prevent the same thing that had happened to her from happening to me. That day in seventh grade, we were on our way home after spring break, and we stopped for gas..."

She stood. What was she saying?

"I babysat the other day for Katie's new baby." That's what she'd meant to say.

Ethan leaned forward. "Cass. What happened when you stopped for gas?"

"Nothing. I don't know why—"

"Cass, they're just words. It's just me. Talk to me. That day in seventh grade, on your way home from spring break, you stopped for gas and..."

She had no idea who she was. "I'd forgotten," she said. Which sounded intentional, or worse, cavalier. She looked past him out the French doors into the darkness and remembered it all, let what had happened that day wash through her, one recovered memory leading to the next, until it was all with her again and the bones in her legs felt bare, exposed. "We stopped for gas. My mother headed inside." She turned, but there was nothing to hold on to, nothing but air around her, nothing to steady her for what she could now see coming. "The air was sweet. There were roses, brilliant reds and yellows, underneath a halo of white. I headed over to read a plaque. *Tended with hope by The Garden Club.*" She looked at Ethan as if he could explain where the words were coming from. "The church bell sounded, and I kneeled on the railroad tie that contained the flower bed. I reached through the wall of leaves to pull a yellow rose toward me. A breeze swirled. It felt good, as if I were being wrapped in a cocoon. I pulled the flower to my nose and inhaled the perfume just as this fluffy black dog ran up to me, his leash dragging. I started to reach for it but this little girl in a yellow dress with my hair, my eyes, my dimples...For a second everything stopped, and we just looked at each other. I thought it was a trick somehow, that I was looking into the past, seeing me.

Then the bell rang out again and a woman screamed. And the dog took off and the little girl after him. And I thought, *yes, run, get away.* I heard the machine-gun sound of a motorcycle. Squealing tires." She wrapped her arms around herself. "Then the thud." Ethan was there, his arms around her. After a moment, she could speak again. She stepped away. "It was so still. A huge black-and-silver motorcycle lay on the asphalt, yellow and red growing out of it into a little girl's dress and bloody caved-in head." Sharp tears cracked off from the depths of some frozen lake, and she let them go, bending over to help them along. Her body heaved with the force of it, and Ethan was there again, standing beside her, his hands on the bones of her hips, holding her in place. She hadn't cried since she was a child. Not when her father died. Not when her mother died. Not that day. Not until this minute when it all came together in front of this man who made her feel safe. Her chest hurt. Her head hurt. Her face ached. Again she stepped away from him, but she felt woozy and reached for the wall. Ethan took a step toward her. She shook her head. "The tiny dog started licking the tiny face and whimpering. The motorcycle driver sat up and collapsed back to the pavement. The wind just kept wrapping around me, white cherry blossom petals floating down." As soft and magical as snowflakes, she remembered now. If only the whole thing could be turned upside down and undone. But it could not. Here it was again, after all these years. And she couldn't stop it. There was more. She looked at Ethan but saw that little girl's mother. " 'Janey, I'm coming,' a pregnant woman cried, and that's when I understood the words she'd been yelling—'Janey, stop! Stop her!' The woman limped by so close I could have reached for her. But I failed to do that, too. Her foot, sliding along behind her, was bent in a way it shouldn't have been. I could have stopped that little girl, Ethan. I heard her mother screaming. I could have saved her. But instead of reaching for the little girl, I turned around to see who was yelling at me."

She took a breath, watching her stomach rise and fall, then watching him.

He turned to the night sky.

After a moment, he started again. "I'm not finished with what I can do in Afghanistan. The people there want so little, and they struggle so mightily for it. Family is vital to them. That's where they get their resilience. There's such potential if they can learn to tear down the walls instead of building them." He turned around to look at her. "To abandon them now would feel the same as if, as if I were abandoning you."

She turned to the night sky.

He came closer, his hands stopping on the back of the sofa. "It's like we struggled so hard to come up with *the agreement*, that once we did, we etched it in stone and nailed it to the front door in between two clocks—mine counting down to nothing and yours up to everything."

She stood and faced him, unable to speak. "Nothing? That's how you see us and what your life will be like if you stay here? I thought you wanted *more* than Afghanistan. I thought you wanted me."

"I didn't mean that the way it sounded. I'm sorry. *You* are not nothing. *We* are not nothing." He exhaled and his voice softened. "I'm not saying what I feel is fair." He came around to the front of the sofa. "I'm saying this is how I feel. I'm the one who's been getting what I wanted. You're the one who's been waiting for your turn. I know. But I just don't think either of us—"

"It was your damn idea."

"I know, Cass, but we were both working to figure it out. I'm just saying...In my world, time is running out. In yours, well, your world is—"

"About to be our world." She curled up onto the sofa. "And now you're saying that's not what you want."

"No, Cass, what I'm trying to say, and saying very badly, is it's taken a toll neither of us expected."

"I don't know whether you're ever going to stay home," she said, more to herself than to him. But then she lifted her head and said slowly and clearly, "You know, if we have a baby, it will never be just the two of us again."

He leaned against the wall, closing his eyes. "I'm giving up everything for you."

Cass felt small, and she hunched over. She had a thin scab on her knee and ran her finger over its rough crust, then she dug her nail in. Nothing. She sat up and reached for a pillow, which she placed over her heart. She was older. And stronger. *You are stronger than me.* And she was. She would not go through that again. The second half of her life would not be a mirror of the first.

"If you really feel that you're giving up everything and that your life will be nothing without Afghanistan," she said, looking at the floor and drained of every drop of emotion, "I don't want you to give it up. You'll resent me for it. It would kill us anyway."

The thud of Ethan knocking his head against the wall caused her to turn in his direction, where the sound of his sliding down down down kept her eyes on his, now level with hers. He looked at her as if he were seeing her for the first time in a long time, seeing her like he used to, and his love seeped in around the edges of the pillow, and she could feel him understanding, and she could feel him feeling the pain she couldn't, and she knew he loved her— despite the obstacles lined up in front of them.

"In this moment, I don't want to give up Afghanistan," he said, facing her. "But love reaches back into the past and forward into the future. It's more than one moment. And I love you more than I want the rest of it. I do, Cass. It will always be the two of us. No matter what else there is, or isn't, it will always be the two of us."

With the telling over, despite his words, she could feel darkness in the room with them, darkness waiting for the light to go out. Clutching the pillow, she drew her legs in under her and laid her head against the arm of the sofa.

For a while, that's the way they stayed—Ethan against the wall, Cass with her body drawn in on the sofa. The darkness waiting. Eventually, he sat with her, not as far away as possible. Sometime later, her knees gave way, sending her feet across the middle into his territory. And finally, he leaned over and covered her body with his.

$$\circ \, ^\circ \circ$$

In the early morning, as the dark sky began to lighten, she cracked the doors and fresh air poured in. She brought him a cup of his strong coffee and sat beside him.

"I told you the film project in Kabul is in trouble," he said. "Which is why I've been on the phone with Setara. We're a week, two at most, from seeing it completed, and I want to make sure it is. I'm going back—tonight."

She stared at the steam from his coffee, not moving, waiting for the whole of it. The telling, it appeared, would never be over.

"To be there in person to make sure it happens. And when I get back in a couple of weeks—"

She looked up. The motor of the fridge shut off.

"I'm sorry," he said and leaned toward her, reaching his hand to her arm.

And that was it, the limit to what she could feel. "How did we end up with so much between us?" she asked.

"This is not an ending," he said.

"Why does it feel that way?"

PART FOUR

FIRE

31

This part was familiar—she'd done it a thousand times. The airport doors swallowed Ethan, and she drove home.

By 8:15, she was in bed with a book she kept letting go of. Her phone buzzed with a text. Vee. *How's it going?*

He's gone back.

And then her phone rang. "Whaaaat?" Vee said.

Cass scrunched down in the bed and recounted the story, the words tumbling out.

"Shit," she said. "I'm still at the bar. Come over."

"I'm already in bed."

"Shit," Vee said again.

○ ○ ○

Cass woke confused, to banging. By the light of her cell, she made her way to the door. Vee was waving at the peephole.

"Surprise," she said after Cass opened the door.

"Why are you here? What time is it?" She stepped back so Vee could come in. She turned on a lamp.

Vee shut the door behind her. "I was waiting for the bus— actually put one foot on—and then I stepped off and bought a six-pack of Blue Moon," which she held up before putting down on the wheelbarrow. "I knew you'd tell me not to come unless I just showed up." She raised both arms in victory.

Cass glanced out the French doors, feeling her sadness like the black night sky. She sat on the arm of the sofa.

"C'mon," Vee said. "Let's go."

"I'm not going anywhere, Vee."

"It's only 10:30. Just grab some shoes."

But where shoes would go, her bare feet were making circles on the floor.

At the sound of keys, Cass looked up. "Library?"

Vee smiled.

Excitement flashed but disappeared. Cass knew instantly how much effort Vee had put into trying to come up with something that would make her feel better. "You're the best," she said. "But I'm sunk."

"Well, we'll un-sink you." Vee grabbed two beers, passing one to Cass before she plopped onto the TV sofa.

Cass twisted the top off her beer and stretched out on the fireplace sofa.

"Am I in Ethan's spot or yours?"

"Ethan's." Cass raised her bottle toward Vee's, and they knocked them together. "I'm glad you're here. I don't feel as bad as I did in my bed. Although I *was* asleep."

"I thought we'd set the cards free," Vee said. "I was hoping there would actually be *cards* in those little drawers."

Cass sat up. "Hope—that's what I needed."

Vee sat up.

"Before you got here, I didn't have any hope."

Vee eased back down.

"Damn it," Cass said, smacking the sofa. "That's what I should have named Howell's GoFundMe campaign. *Hope for Howell.*"

"But *Help Howell House* is good, too. Hey, I saw Ethan's photo on the cover of *TIME*. Amazing, as usual."

Their copy was back in the bedroom on the chest of drawers.

"There's so much clarity in this one. And so many layers—the girl trapped inside, the boy leaving the house—a shiver of the future. Inside, outside. Female, male. The colors. But the light shines only on the girl. He's quite something."

"You and I are both married," Cass said, "and neither of us has anyone wondering where we are or waiting for us to come home."

"Which sometimes is nice—that feeling of no one pulling on you."

"Growing up, I got so good at *alone*. Then I got married and thought alone was over. I let my guard down, and now it's hit me all over again. Aren't you lonely?"

"Sometimes," Vee said. "But I'm rereading May Sarton's *Journal of a Solitude*—I love that book—and I refuse to let loneliness have its way."

"Refuse how?"

"Instead of wishing for someone else, I'm trying to think about myself. What would I like to do with this moment? And sometimes the answer is to be with Dillon. But sometimes it's not. Sometimes I would actually like to read or watch a show he doesn't like or eat pie for dinner."

"When you gave me a copy of that book," Cass said, "I thought it was going to be a how-to. A triumph of solitude. That I would find the answer on how to be at peace when I'm by myself. But instead, there was just the struggle. She seems to always be struggling."

" 'There is nothing to be done but go ahead with life moment by moment and hour by hour—put out birdseed, tidy the rooms, try to create order and peace around me even if I cannot achieve it inside me.' That's kind of how-to."

"Not in my world," Cass said.

"Life is not really as black-and-white as we would like it to be."

"Half his heart is over there."

"I wish I knew where the rest of Dillon's was. I guess I do. In a bottle."

"Do you think you might get back together?" Cass asked.

Vee pushed herself to sitting, pulling her knees to her chest. "When he's not drinking, he's the same Dillon I fell in love with. But he's usually drinking."

"Do you ever see him?" Cass asked.

Vee shook her head. "But I told him he could call or text if it helped. Sometimes he's in a really bad way, and it takes all I have. He starts talking, and I start right back loving him. His voice is thick, like country music. Even after we hang up, he keeps on spreading through me."

"This isn't the way it was supposed to be," Cass said.

Vee got quiet. "I'm super afraid, you know. That's why I have to go after it. Otherwise it would tear me apart."

Cass flipped around so she was facing Vee.

"It feels like I'm just waiting to see what happens next," Vee said.

"Me, too," Cass said.

"I need to tell you something." Vee hesitated. "Two months ago, Dillon came home worse drunk than usual. I got mad. He said I wasn't going to tell him what he could do. And then he hit me."

"Oh, Vee," Cass said, sitting up.

"He hit me over and over again."

Cass didn't move.

"He's not much bigger than me, and I would have thought, if it had ever occurred to me, that I could defend myself better than I was able to. I cut my forehead on the corner of a table as I fell." She touched the scar above her eye. "My nose was swollen for days."

Vee's tears slipped over the edge of her lids and down her face. Cass had forgotten about the scar.

"At some point, Singer and his mother came in. I had been screaming, they told me later. His mother and I keep each other's keys since we live right next door. Singer happened to be eating with her that night, and he pulled Dillon off me and shoved him against the wall. Which was apparently all Dillon needed to break out of whatever trance he was in. When he saw me, bleeding on the floor, he fell apart. The cops arrived soon after, and the paramedics. Singer's mom rode with me in the ambulance. He followed behind." Vee looked at her. "It was the worst moment of my life. I was so scared. And I don't think I fought back at all."

"I'm so sorry," Cass said.

"But...more women are killed by their partner *after* they have separated than while still together."

"Oh, God."

"So I got a restraining order. He's not allowed to come to the apartment or the library. Or within a thousand yards of me. He wouldn't anyway. He's too ashamed of what he did. And scared he might do it again. Because he never would have thought he would have done it the first time. I still love him. And I'm ashamed of that."

A heat began to travel through Cass's body, starting at her feet and crawling up, until her cheeks felt splotchy red and her body felt prickly. She wanted to tell Vee what else she'd remembered about the accident, but even thinking *what else* reduced it to mere detail when it was everything...It would all be too much. She reached up to pull on her ears, to try to stop the buzzing.

"Now love is all mixed up in shame, and he's so sweet on the phone, and I can't seem to move forward. And I don't want people feeling sorry for me. You're the first person I've told."

Vee seemed calmer, her skin less puffy. Her hand was on the back of the sofa, and Cass covered it with hers.

"Well, I've managed to make a sad situation even sadder," she said. "That's a real accomplishment for me."

"Stop," Cass said. But it was true. Vee usually avoided sad at all costs.

The bird was sneaking out of Vee's sleeve. "I go back and forth. Is it one bird in motion? Or is it a flock? What do you see when you look at it?"

"Upside down birds."

Cass laughed.

"Yeah, I didn't think that through all the way."

32

Red blankets and a ruby red rug. A red tray full of eyeglasses on the coffee table. A red bookshelf full of hats. Under the window, red heels crowned a slender table.

Cass held her coffee with two hands and balanced her computer on her lap. Lois was helping her with the second mass mailing, the letter she'd started but abandoned. At the end of June, she would meet with the Woodruff Foundation. The first week in July, her meetings with major donors would begin.

"This is what I've come to," Lois said. "The things in this room. But these are the things that make me happy. My red shoes are like the hot fudge on top of the sundae." She took a sip from her red mug of tea, then put it down on the tray in front of her next to the measuring cup half full of cream.

"Not the cherry?" Cass said.

"I could eat a sundae without a cherry and be perfectly happy. But I have no interest in a sundae without hot fudge."

"Me neither," Cass said.

"I didn't understand that—that the red shoes were holding it all together, that the red shoes I didn't wear anymore would make all the difference."

Which made Cass think of Lois's son. "Are you glad you had children?" Cass asked, before she remembered she was done with this subject.

Lois looked at her. "I got married when I was nineteen because my mother told me the good guys were grabbed up early. I had kids because that was the next thing. Not for one minute did I think about what my life would be like. Or alternative lives. Or what kind of life I wanted. By that time, the children were standing in front of me, and they needed to get to piano practice. I just put my head down and did it. Then there were grandchildren to get to know."

"But...no planning?" Cass said.

"No planning," Lois said. "Maybe that would have made things better, but I doubt it. I had friends who planned, but life never seems to go the way one expects. And even if it does, people change and want different things. But children are a lot of fun. That's the trick—to find the pleasure in the unexpected."

"May said something similar." Cass looked around. "It sure is nice sitting here in your red room."

"Hey," Lois said, picking up the letter Cass had brought in. "That's what you need to focus on in the letter. There's something about a home. Bedrooms upstairs, a kitchen and a den. Lives crossing and bouncing off each other. Windows to open and doors that lead to yards where we can sit and listen to the birds. I didn't want to live by myself or in one of those places that feels like a hotel or a hospital. Staying at my son's house felt as if I was intruding on the life he was supposed to have, and as if everything was his to decide. I felt like I should be grateful for something I didn't want. That sounds harsh, but there you go. It's the truth. Maybe Atta is rubbing off on me. But here...here there's so much to look forward to each day. It's so alive. This lovely red room belongs to me. I can read all day if that's what I want. And sometimes I even look forward to talking to Atta."

$$\circ \, {}^{\circ} \, \circ$$

Down the hall, May's door was cracked. Cass knocked and pushed it open.

"Good gosh, what happened?"

In her black yoga pants and a big white T-shirt, May looked up at her. "I couldn't remember the last time I sat on the floor. There's so much space down here." Her little legs spilled out in front of her.

Cass sat down beside her. "Did you fall, May?"

"I held onto the bedpost and lowered myself down. It was intentional. Do you see my boxes? I caught an edge of them but now I can't find them."

Cass located the boxes and stretched to reach them. A stack of three in different sizes, each one covered in flowered paper. She scooted them in front of May and put May's hands on them.

"They're like the three bears, aren't they?" May said, giggling. "Papa bear, Mama bear, and Baby bear." She took the top off the smallest one, which was full of pieces of paper. Her notes. "My little windows. Will you read one to me?"

Cass reached into the box and pulled out a small blue paper and unfolded it. "See you tonight, honey."

May lit up.

"And there's a heart."

"Some days I miss Harvey. I always liked knowing he was there. You think it will be forever, a carpet that will never stop unrolling. But even if you're lucky, the 'two of you' ends. Another one?"

From the bottom of the box, Cass pulled out a white paper with a torn edge. "I left my toothbrush so you'd know I was coming back."

"Oh, my," May said. "That might be the first note he ever left me."

"And there's a heart."

"Always a heart." May hugged the boxes to her chest. "Isn't this great?"

"It is." Cass smiled. "Would you like to look in the other boxes?"

"The biggest one has photos, you know. And Mama bear holds letters and cards, and a key or two. Harvey was always keeping the keys to hotel rooms we stayed in and giving them to me when we got home." Her brow furrowed. She looked through the open door into the distance of the hall. "But I need to get up off the floor before I petrify in this position. And I want to think on that old toothbrush for a while."

○ ○ ○

Over time, the Fates changed. When Cass had first volunteered, it had been May, Vivian, and Clara. Clara with the moplike hair, as if she never brushed it. Her perpetually arched eyebrows. She saw the world in colors and had been Cass's first experience with dementia. One afternoon, Cass had searched for her for hours, finally finding her at dusk in a little playground off Church Street a mile and a half away, sitting at the bottom of a shiny yellow slide.

"Clara," she had called from across the street, waving.

Clara had looked up but hadn't moved. When Cass reached her, she threw her arms around her, but Clara kept hold of the end of the slide.

"I found it," she said, with no change of expression. "This is where the sun pours out."

In that moment, Cass saw her own mother—her absence of joy, the way she stared ahead but saw nothing, not even Cass. And for just a second, Cass could imagine loving her mother the way she loved Clara. Then it was gone, but she'd felt it.

Sitting on the ground, Cass had placed her hand on Clara's foot, calling Clara's daughter and Howell House. Like Ruth Ann, who preceded Lois, Clara had not been allowed back at Howell, but Cass had felt good about their time there. And when Clara left, a spot opened up for Ruby—Ruby with her red hair and house dresses, whose answer to every question was *you pick*.

○ ○ ○

Cass dropped her computer and notes and coffee mug on her desk, but she wasn't ready to sit back down. In the living room, she stood by the window where she'd first talked to May, but this time she looked in at the room where Hattie's two pale yellow loveseats faced each other in front of the fireplace below the portrait of Betsy

Ross sewing the flag, a woman assisting on each side. Cass would find the money. She had to.

Back at her desk, she worked late, writing letter after letter after letter to everyone she could think of, telling them story after story about Clara and Ruth Ann and Atta and Lois and May and this amazing place that needed only money to survive—all the while listening to the sounds of the Fates coming down to dinner and then heading back up, not one of them using the elevator. But if Cass paused for a sip of water or to think of the right word, it was the image of Clara that evening at the slide that she saw, and she was overcome by the golden feeling of something fading away rather than beginning, a sunset instead of a sunrise, that moment of gratitude before darkness sets in.

33

Light flooded the room, but Cass lay in bed, staring at the white ceiling. At seven, her alarm went off and the phone rang—both at the same time.

"Happy birthday, babe."

"Thanks." Her head fell back on the pillow.

"I'm sorry I'm not there."

"Yeah, me, too."

"I'll be home soon."

"Okay."

"You don't sound too good."

"What did you expect?"

"Cass, I'm sorry."

"I know."

"We'll celebrate when I get home."

"Thanks for calling."

$$\circ \, {}^{\circ} \, \circ$$

Cass and Vee headed down the front steps of the library. "I guess that's the end of Tidal Flats."

"Maybe he'll just be a few days late," Vee said, dropping her keys into her purse. "And, the truth is, the agreement doesn't blow up just because he's not home on the exact day."

"It doesn't bode well."

"I'll give you that," Vee said.

Cars raced by so close that Cass's hair floated away from her head, so close the sidewalk felt like another lane, all the husbands and wives in a hurry to get home.

"He called this morning to wish me a happy birthday," she said. "It was nothing but sad."

"Well," Vee said, as she opened the door to Bacchanalia where they were going to celebrate, "nothing but fun now."

$$\circ \, ^{\circ} \circ$$

After dinner, on the door to the apartment, a note. *Cassie, Was in the neighborhood. Happy Birthday! Love Wheeler.*

No comma after love. *Love Wheeler.* She did love Wheeler. His ex-wife was probably the only person in the world who didn't love him.

In the bedroom, she picked up their most recent copy of *TIME*, the one with Ethan's photo on the cover and turned to "The Story Behind the Photo," the story she couldn't get out of her head.

I was with my fixer, Baquir, my business partner, Setara Ali, and her husband, Feda Ali. The four of us were headed to our warehouse in Karte-Char when Setara called my name. I turned, confused for a moment as I didn't see her. But of course, she was wearing a burka. I followed her nod and then the scent of baking bread and spice—a young girl's face framed in a window. Somehow, I had missed the curious eyes trapped inside. I began to shoot, changing positions, aware of the overcast day, the intermittent sun, the window glass. My hands were sweating, but I waited, hoping for an opposing force, something that would pull the moment in more than one direction. I was waiting for the thing that didn't have to be there, that usually isn't there as I begin. The young girl was looking out through square panes. Next to the window was a blue door. I moved in an arc, by inches, varying the zoom and the angle, shot after shot as the day seemed frozen. Her face, her life, and then a man pushing a yellow wheelbarrow in front of the blue door. Steady, I told myself. The door opened, and a young boy in a red shirt, two books at his side, entered the viewfinder and stepped down, passing in front of the window. I had the shot.

○ ○ ○

In "The After Photo" at the bottom of the page, the light had changed, as if the sun had disappeared behind a cloud. Feda was crushing his cigarette under his shoe, Baquir was bowing so slightly she almost missed it—it was just the pitch of his head, his downturned eyes—and Setara had already turned and was continuing down the street.

○ ○ ○

Thirty. Alone in bed in a room of unsettling darkness, the only light a line underneath her closet door. She'd left the light on by accident, and now illuminated was that safe dark of so long ago. She could see it all. The glass knob she could barely reach, the big door popping open, the scratchy rug, pulling the door closed behind her, the swoosh of dresses, the cool forest, burrowing in to look for the talking elephants who would tear the darkness to shreds. The darkness that was always there, and always waiting for the light to go out.

She flattened her pillow and pulled the thin spring covers over her shoulders all the way up to her neck. Underneath the darkness was where she slept.

But out here, above her, there were no dresses, only emptiness. Too much space. And the darkness felt as if it were swirling around trying to fill every inch of it. This was the first birthday since they'd met that she'd celebrated without Ethan. It was the day before their anniversary. They were always together for both.

On Ethan's bedside table, the clock ticked. Not quite ten. She glanced around the room, wanting something. Something sweet. Ice cream. The market would still be open. She turned on the light and threw on one of Ethan's old white button-downs and hopped into her jeans. Then she remembered he'd called that morning. There was no need to hurry.

$$\circ \, {}^{\circ} \, \circ$$

Light spilled out the front windows of the market, but inside it was manageable. She could see it all in one go—its two rooms veering off like wings held together by one cash register. Instead of walls, white wooden, recessed shelves went to the ceiling, each shelf shallow so that nothing could hide behind anything else, reassuring her of the sturdiness of the world.

Two pints of Ben & Jerry's. Once outside, she pried the top off one and dug in with the plastic spoon she'd found by the drink machine, eating as she headed back to her apartment, the ice cream definitely making her feel better. She slowed by the bar but didn't stop. As she stepped onto the bridge, the door creaked open behind her. "It's the birthday girl."

She turned, and her mouth full, lifted the open container.

"What kind is it?" Singer asked, making his way to the bridge.

"Imagine Whirled Peace," she said, laughing. "Want a bite?"

"I'll definitely have some of that."

She dipped the spoon into the carton and slid it into his mouth. He placed his hand on hers. Their eyes met. And seconds later, the spoon was still in his mouth, and she was still holding onto it, and his hand was still on hers, and the ice cream was surely gone.

"It *is* good," he said, after she managed to take her hand back. "I usually go with Cherry Garcia."

Cass concentrated on closing up the quart and dropping it and the spoon in the bag. Singer cleared his throat and looked straight ahead. But they were still inside something.

"I'll walk you home," he said. "I certainly don't want anything to happen to you on your birthday."

She swallowed, confused about what she wanted, unable to take her eyes off the soft spot underneath the shoulder blade of this man walking ahead of her, within her reach.

He turned, and started to say something, then paused.

"What?" she said.

"I'm sure Ethan wishes he could be here."

"He could have been."

A breeze lifted pieces of Singer's rich red hair. His green eyes were full of light. Warm, that's how he felt. And he was here now when she was owed someone here now.

But she didn't want warm; she wanted Ethan.

34

The sound of darkness, the phone ringing in the middle of the night.

"Is this the residence of Mr. Ethan Graham?"

"Yes," Cass said, into the dark.

"Is this Mary Cassatt Miller?"

"Yes," she said again, her heart throwing her forward, her feet searching for the floor.

"This is the deputy ambassador calling from the United States Embassy in Afghanistan."

"What happened?"

"I'm sorry, but I have to inform you that Mr. Ethan Graham has been reported missing. We've notified the US State Department, and we are doing everything we can to locate him."

"Couldn't he just be traveling?" He followed the photos. He could be anywhere.

"The provincial security chief of Bamiyan province reported him missing a couple of hours ago. We have confirmed he is not at the boarding house where he was staying."

She turned on the light, squinting at its abruptness, too bright and not bright enough. She grabbed a pen.

"We will call again when we have more information."

"Wait," she said. "Can we set a time you'll call back?"

"Just a moment."

The muffled voices—two, maybe three—speaking a language she didn't understand were closer to Ethan than she was.

"We will call again in three hours."

She looked at the clock—5:15 a.m. She asked for a name and a number. *Don't go*, she wanted to say. But there was the click and the dial tone. The sound of no one.

Now that she'd hung up, it was quiet again. If she turned out the light, lay down, and went back to sleep, except for the scribbling on the pad beside her, everything in this room would be the same.

She stood. Then she sat again. She pinched her arm to see if she could feel it. She was supposed to do something if this happened, but she couldn't remember what. *Think.*

Wheeler.

He answered as if he'd been waiting for the phone to ring. "Ethan..."

"Cass?"

"Wheeler, he's missing."

"Jesus."

"The embassy said they'd notified the State Department, and that they'd call back in three hours."

"I'll be right there."

"It's our anniversary," she said as she realized it, sinking onto the bed, breathing out, her breath emerging not as air but as ache.

"It's going to be okay, Cass."

But when she hung up, the darkness seemed stronger; Ethan's side of the bed, emptier. On his night table, the face of their clock was dark to match the sky, but there was the tick forward.

In the bathroom, she turned on the shower full force. She was out and dressed in minutes.

Coffee.

In the kitchen, she tried to stand and wait but couldn't. Instead, she walked up and down the hall until she was sure the machine was ready, then when the coffee was, she drank from her cup, burning her tongue with force and intention.

35

Wheeler placed two mugs of milky coffee on the dining room table as he settled into the chair beside her. He'd arrived in a worn leather jacket against the cool of the early May morning, his broad middle and outstretched arms a nest. She warmed her hands around the mug and eyed his setup—two computers, a small printer, his phone, a yellow pad in front of him, a pen in his hand.

"Have you done this before?" she asked.

He squeezed her hand, and she sunk her teeth into her tongue so she wouldn't cry.

"I have," he said. "Don't worry. Ethan could just be lying low. But being taken is a risk in a war zone. He knew that. You knew that. We all know it."

But she didn't know it like this.

"Kidnapping's become something of an industry in Afghanistan. It's not as mysterious a thing as it is in the States. I know CNN is backing their project. Ethan and I talked about it, but I've been gone the last two weeks. Tell me what you know about what he was doing."

Inhaling, she nodded. "He and Setara...." And she paused, watching Ethan's best friend for any small change in expression, but Wheeler didn't roll his eyes, or fidget, or look away. "He and Setara are working on the project to put cameras in the hands of the Afghans so they can speak for themselves...But the Afghan government has been trying to stop them. They've arrested a couple of their people. They closed down the first place they were meeting. Somebody died. Ethan was unsure if it was intentional." She grabbed hold of her knees. "I told him it was too dangerous to go back." She shivered. "But he was so excited about teaching them to take photos."

"I'll make it warmer in here," he said, hopping up.

She put her hand out to stop him. "Stay."

Sitting back down, he asked, "Do you know where he was?"

"Kabul, I think." She looked at Wheeler. "I don't know." Should she have known? "Wait, the deputy ambassador mentioned Bamiyan province. That's who reported him missing, the provincial security chief there."

As Wheeler typed into his computer, he asked when she'd talked to him the last time, but the ding of a new email interrupted.

"My guy at CNN says the AP is reporting it." Wheeler stared at the screen before angling it toward her. He stood beside her. She felt his hand on her shoulder.

KABUL, Afghanistan (AP)—*As the last American combat troops prepare to leave Afghanistan, the US Embassy in Kabul reports that American photojournalist Ethan Graham is missing. Also missing is Setara Ali, a leader in the Revolutionary Association of the Women of Afghanistan (RAWA), an Afghan women's rights organization, and the woman behind the face of Graham's famous* TIME *cover of* The Afghan Woman.

"At least he's not alone," she said. Then she stood and drifted to the French doors. Nothing but thick layers of clouds. No sun anywhere. It was so still.

36

Wheeler got off his cell. "CNN has contacted the risk-management team. They're standing by."

"Does that mean they think it's a kidnapping?"

He shook his head. "He's officially missing. So, we notify them."

Missing sounded as if he might not be anywhere. It sounded almost worse than *kidnapped*. She shook her head, trying to clear it.

The landline. Cass ran for the bedroom, Wheeler behind her. "*The Atlanta-Journal Constitution*," she said, the receiver dangling from her finger.

Wheeler caught the phone and after a minute said, "We don't know anything more than that." He hung up, detached the phone cord, untangled it, plugged it back in, and stretched it across her unmade side of the bed, the white sheets every which way. Indentations. But it didn't reach, the phone disappearing into the sheets.

"Do you have another jack out there?"

"Ethan did the phone," she said, leaning against the bedroom door. "For 911. So they could tell what apartment a call was coming from." But the call this morning hadn't come from inside.

Wheeler grabbed a book—Rumi—from her desk and laid it on the rough covers, propping the phone on top of it. Next to her messy side, Ethan's untouched side. Half here, half gone. That quickly the bedroom no longer felt safe. She turned and headed down the hall, pulling her cell out of her pocket. When Vee answered, Cass felt a swelling underneath her lids. Something fell in her chest.

"Cass?" she said again.

Like a child worried that saying the words would make them come true, she hesitated. Then in a whisper that left her no air, she said, "Ethan's missing."

"I'm on my way," Vee said.

As Cass emerged from the narrow hallway into the open den, she stood by Wheeler's setup not knowing what to do or where to be. By the front door, Ethan's blue chair from Afghanistan—which she fell into, drawing her legs up underneath her as her face landed on the rough fabric, nose first, as if she could inhale him right out of wherever he was. *Breathe*, she told herself.

37

The voice on the other end of the phone asked her to hold for the ambassador, but she couldn't hold. She couldn't wait anymore, not for news she couldn't bear. Again, she left it to Wheeler who introduced himself and then propped the receiver between his ear and his shoulder as he pulled a small pad from his back pocket and began to make notes. Cass felt the gray walls closing in and heard her father's voice, telling her to move, to do something, but what she wanted was to crawl back into the rumpled sheets and pull them over her head. Instead, she slid to the floor right at Wheeler's feet. He crouched beside her, then he sat, his knees a makeshift desk, the bed a chair-back, his shoulder to her shoulder.

When he hung up, he said, "The ambassador is calling it a kidnapping. Ethan was taken about twelve hours ago, in the early morning."

Taken.

"It sounds worse than it is."

She looked at him.

"It happened in a national park in the middle of nowhere, about three and a half hours outside of Kabul. The kidnappers also took Ethan's van. The Afghans he was with—working on the camera project—had to find a ride out of the park to Bamiyan. The police in Bamiyan detained them without notifying anyone. Now they're on their way back to the embassy in Kabul. We should know more shortly."

"A national park?"

"Band-e-Amir," he said. "Outside of Bamiyan. Deep blue lakes. I saw them once. Unforgettable. I guess they were there to practice taking photos."

Ethan had deep blue eyes, unforgettable.

"Is anyone claiming responsibility?" The words felt fake in her mouth. She only knew to ask from the news.

Wheeler shook his head.

"Have they asked for money?"

He shook his head again. "That's all the ambassador knows. He'll call back after he talks to the guys who were with Ethan. I've got to call CNN."

"What about Baquir?" she asked, but the doorbell rang, and she sprang for it.

"Are you okay?" Vee asked, throwing her arms around Cass, saying, "He's going to be fine."

Cass wanted people to keep saying this.

Vee dropped her purse on the wheelbarrow and approached Wheeler. They introduced themselves.

"Do you know anything yet?" Vee asked him.

He passed her the AP article he'd printed.

"Oh, God," she said, looking at Cass. "Setara, too?"

Cass nodded and lunged for the French doors, which she opened wide. She was frantic for air. Vee squeezed in beside her on the narrow balcony. Earlier, it had seemed so still, but now the wind was everywhere, throwing their hair back and forth.

"It was so weird when the call came in this morning. After I hung up, the world around me was just the same. No funnel cloud, no siren, no destruction. It was hard to know what was real. I thought maybe if I turned out the light and lay back down, it would all go away. It felt like standing on the edge of a cliff, like I couldn't trust myself."

Behind them, Wheeler's cell rang, but he was talking low and staring into his computer. The landline rang again, and Wheeler said he'd get it, his cell still by his ear.

"It felt like it was up to me to keep him from being swallowed up," Cass said. "But of course, it wasn't. It's not."

Vee leaned into her, and Cass leaned back.

Now the sky was a mess of oddly shaped clouds racing by—no more defined layers. Way to the left, a light gray cloud in the shape of a heart. Cass kept her eye on it as it sailed across the piece of sky she could see. She kept her eye on it, watching as it disappeared.

38

Wheeler called her name, and she stepped back inside.

"We have a few more pieces of the puzzle."

She sat in one of the chairs in front of the window. Vee sat in the other one.

Wheeler crouched beside her. "That was the State Department. They've been in touch with the American Embassy. Our ambassador has talked directly to the Afghans who were with Ethan when he was taken. They took Baquir, too, and Qasem, a young man Ethan and Setara were teaching—he's the one they think caused the problem. It turns out, in addition to photos, Ethan and Setara's group was at Band-e-Amir to interview the first female park rangers in Afghanistan."

"Why would Ethan be doing that?" Then she knew of course.

"They started the interviews the day before and spent the night. The plan was for an early hike to the top of the mountain to take photos of the sunrise. When they went to their van around 4:30 a.m. for their cameras, armed gunman surrounded them. When the captors tried to take the cameras, Setara fought back and they beat her up. The ambassador thinks the police were in on it. Qasem had been bragging about the cameras, and some of the residents were not so excited about the female park rangers."

They were both looking at her.

"Are you okay?" Vee asked. "Have you eaten anything?"

"I've forgotten all about work." But she didn't move. She felt socked in.

"I'll call Ella," Vee said, making her way toward the kitchen.

When Vee came back, she brought Cass a glass of water, a bowl of nuts, and a banana, and when the landline rang the next time, she said she would just stay back there to answer it. Wheeler picked up one of his larger yellow pads and headed that way. Cass went along behind him.

Vee was making Cass's side of the bed. Wheeler stopped at the door, and Cass stopped in the hallway by the kitchen, each looking ahead and watching. Since the call from Afghanistan this morning, she'd been afraid and worried, but this was the first moment she'd missed Ethan, missed him standing in the bedroom while she watched him answer the phone or pick up a book or stare into the dark. It made her heart ache, and she rubbed it, leaning against the wall.

When Wheeler came out, he led her back to the sofa. "Sit here until you finish this glass of water and eat this banana."

"It's dark now, over there," she said. "He's been missing the whole day."

"We're going to get him back."

"Wheeler," Vee called from the bedroom.

"Eat," he told Cass, as he headed down the hall.

She concentrated on swallowing.

A minute later, Vee came and sat beside her. "He's talking to the State Department again."

Cass took another bite of banana, just like she was supposed to. Maybe if she did what she was supposed to, this would all turn out okay. She wondered if she would have to want a baby for this to turn out okay.

Wheeler came into the den. "Does red tape on a camera mean anything to you?"

She threw her arm across her chest to hold herself together, then turned to face Wheeler. "Ethan's cameras," she said. "The ones he uses have red tape on them."

"Since when?" Wheeler asked.

"This trip."

"Okay," he said. "Back in a minute."

The banana seemed faded, more white than yellow. But like an obedient child, she put it in her mouth. Too soft. Way too soft.

He came right back. "The kidnappers are asking for money."

She gagged but managed to swallow the mash of banana back down again. Vee rubbed her back.

"This is good," he said. "If they don't ask for money right away, you worry they're selling the hostages up the food chain to one of the more established groups. Who would then transfer them across the border into Pakistan and to the Taliban."

"How much?" Cass asked.

"Five hundred thousand for Ethan and two fifty for Setara."

Setara.

"What about Baquir?"

"He's the one who delivered the message."

Cass kicked at the brick around the fireplace. "We don't have that much money."

"CNN will pay, not you. And they will offer less than that."

Cass stood.

"Standard practice. Every kidnapping is about control. To offer less is to take back some control. The kidnappers would rather have *some* money."

Than what? She sank to the sofa.

"They will agree on an amount, and CNN will put up the money. There's insurance."

"Kidnapping insurance?"

"K&R coverage," Wheeler said. And then he looked as if he were going to say something else, but he didn't.

The phone rang again, and Vee headed back to her post in the bedroom. Wheeler got on his cell. Cass felt as if she were drowning and was surprised to find herself still on the sofa. Her skin was starting to hurt. She didn't want CNN to help Setara. And she didn't want that thought in her head. But there it was. She stood again. Of course, she wanted CNN to help Setara. She just wanted them to help Ethan first or more. Jeez, she didn't want anything bad to happen to anyone.

Wheeler slid his phone into his pocket. "I'm going to run over to the CNN offices to see if I can speed this along. The crisis management people are on site. We need to work fast."

"I don't want you to go," she said.

For a second, he just stared at her. "Vee's here."

"Right," she said, as if she had momentarily forgotten. But Wheeler was comforting in a way that Vee was not.

When the front door shut, Cass stood there staring at it. She wondered if Ethan were afraid but could not imagine it. Beyond the French doors, the sky seemed frozen in place. Inching the doors open, she slid sideways through the small space she'd created. She breathed in the horns and screeches, the sirens, trying to loosen her limbs and allow her body to soften, to take up more room instead of as little as possible. But when she felt the wind pushing her, she tensed and pushed back.

39

In the bedroom, Vee sat on the floor, looking at Rumi.

"I've never actually read this before. It's amazing. I love this part you underlined. *You have escaped the cage. Your wings / are stretched out. Now, fly.*"

Cass stepped around her to lie on the bed. She turned on her side, toward Vee. "That's my father's book. His underlinings."

"Your father was a cool dude."

The phone rang. Vee answered, then said, "No comment," and hung up. "I now know the AIP is the Afghan Islamic Press."

Cass sat up.

"Did I hear Wheeler leave?" Vee asked.

"He went over to CNN," she said, standing, "to see if he could hurry the money thing along."

Vee glanced toward the door. "He seems like he would do anything for you," she said, leaning back against the bed.

"He just met you, and he'd do anything for you, too. He's a hundred percent love and support. I don't know anyone else like him." Cass shook her hands in the air. "I keep thinking maybe Ethan will call."

"He might."

"He says Afghans don't even flinch at gunfire, that it could be a few blocks away, and they just keep crossing the street. There's only one area in Kabul where he'll even go out at night."

The phone rang. Vee answered and shook her head. Out their wall of windows, again Cass followed a cloud from one pane to the next, but soon it was gone. She wanted something that didn't move, something she could latch on to. Brick. Granite. Wood. Her desk. In a small dish in one corner, the bullet, and she reached for it.

Vee hung up. "Is that what I think it is?"

"From a long time ago," Cass said. "Right after we got married. He got shot in the back. It wasn't serious." She made a fist around it, enclosed it. "I knew he was okay before I knew he'd been hurt."

"It's scary how something so small can do so much damage."

"While Ethan was being kidnapped, I was with Singer." She wrapped her arms around herself.

"Oh, Cass."

"It was nothing. He saw me getting ice cream and walked me home. It's just, I was with him."

Vee put down her pad and extended her legs.

Cass opened her fist and looked at the bullet. "Ethan gave me this to help me remember he could survive anything, and that I could, too. That we could."

The doorbell rang.

Cass looked at Vee.

Vee hopped up. "I'll get it."

Cass folded into Vee's place on the floor, but she leaned hard against her desk, forcing the brass handles into her back, inching sideways to feel the sharp line of a corner.

As Wheeler, then Vee, came into the room, she held tight to the bullet that had once been inside Ethan, and she looked from one to the other, feeling like a kid with her parents standing over her, and yet she never remembered that actually happening. Wheeler came and squatted next to her. "They've agreed on an amount, and CNN's working on the money. The wire instructions are coming any minute."

"Is this going to work?" Cass asked.

"The ambassador thinks so, unofficially, that is. The risk managers agree. The area where Ethan was taken is not a stronghold of the insurgency, so they're probably just hostage takers. Plus they asked for money."

"Unofficially?"

"Officially, we don't negotiate with terrorists."

Wheeler helped her up and headed back to his computer. Vee answered the phone. Cass slid the bullet into her jeans pocket and wandered down the hall. As she came into the den, Wheeler said, "The money's on its way."

She stood beside him. "Is it going to the embassy?"

He shook his head slowly.

She remembered. Unofficially.

"I hope you trust Baquir," he said. "Anyway, I know Ethan does."

Of course, Ethan trusted Baquir. Ethan trusted her, too.

"The National Directorate of Security, the Afghan intelligence service, is working with Baquir, but he's taking the money in."

She sat next to Wheeler.

"And we're wiring money for Setara, too," he said.

"Good," she said. That was settled. She looked toward Ethan's photos. Almost noon here. Almost eight thirty at night there.

Wheeler put his hands on his knees. "Now we wait."

40

Hours passed, the sun lost its power, the rooms turned stale. Wheeler was on a first-name basis with the United States Ambassador to Afghanistan. *Jim.* Then the phone quieted, and Vee left to pick up food.

Cass went back to the bedroom and sat at her desk. When she was a kid, her dolls had collected dust, but her desk had always shined. Her father liked to put his hand on it and say, *from my great-grandmother to my grandfather to my mother to me to you.* When she would ask for the story of the fire, he would describe his great-grandmother, a teenager at the time, as she stood on a hill on a cold, starless night, her long, white nightgown billowing in the wind that was fanning the fire, screaming over and over for her desk until two neighbors bashed a window and hauled it out. The house had burned to the ground, but the desk had survived. The story of the fire, he would say, is the story of the desk.

Her father always stood with both feet planted. He never leaned. He read Rumi and flew jets. He loved her mother, and he loved her. When he was home, her mother was happy, and no matter what was going on, he would come into her room to tell her goodnight, lifting a handle on this desk, then letting it fall. Three times, always. And each time, it would jangle like a bell. He would sit on her bed, and she would roll toward him, grabbing the edges of the mattress to stop herself. With the wall on one side and her father on the other, she felt safe. After the jangling came the tickling, and after the tickling came the part where he rested his hand on top of her head. And finally, the part where she said, *I wish you were here every night.*

Cass opened the bottom drawer on the left. *Dear Lulu,* the

letter began. Her father had started calling her "Lulu" when she was in ninth grade, when she first parted her hair in the middle. It had been longer then and even straighter. He'd told her she was the spitting image of a Scottish actress from the sixties.

Dear Lulu,

Snow has been falling for eight hours now, since about lunchtime. At first it only stuck in a few places, melting on the tarmac and roads. I thought it wouldn't amount to much. But it didn't quit. Hour after hour, flake after flake until it began to accumulate. Then the snowplow came along. But the snow just seemed more determined than ever. I stepped out of the barracks an hour ago, and all you can see is white. Even the air is white. The snowplow passes, but it's no match for the tiny flakes. Isn't that something? Now it's dark, and yet it's all white everywhere. I'm thinking about going out and kicking it around a bit, but at the same time, I don't really want to disturb it.

It's a white world. Your mother would have loved it.

See you in a few weeks.

Love, Dad

But she never saw him again.

She folded her father's letter and put it back where it belonged. Her father had sent her so many, and she'd thought there would always be more. When he died, she only had this one. If something happened to Ethan, it would have been six days since they had touched.

Cass opened the bottom drawer on the right. A stack of Ethan's letters. She'd had to beg him to write, had had to confess the whole story of her father's letters. Only then had he said he would. She unfolded one written on rough, homemade paper.

Dear Cass,

Right now I'm trapped in a square box of a room. Just me and the dust and heat and this stillness. That's what I notice, the quiet, not the gunfire. Two hours of winding this way and that through the mountains to get here from Kabul, past crazy-colored Pakistani trucks, decrepit pickups full of wheelbarrows, and convoys of American military with gunners on top.

There are sheets at the windows to hide me from the neighbors or at least to prevent them from constantly being reminded I'm here. Three long, narrow, churchlike windows—a slightly larger one flanked by two smaller ones. And sheets on my pallet in the corner.

A minute ago, I turned out the light and risked a glance. Minus the smoke from the explosions, I could be in southern France. The rolling hills, the flat-roofs of earth-toned houses. Low gray clouds lit pink on the underside by the sun on its way down over the distant mountains. The smell of grilling meat. Invisible particles of dust peppering my skin.

This fancy light fixture in the middle of the ceiling follows me from corner to corner. A gold, four-leafed flower in the center of an unpainted ceiling. It doesn't belong here.

The beginning of my beard itches.

There's a bunch of red rugs that cover the floor and crawl up the barely green walls. One of the rugs has a blue-black elephant foot design. I have no idea what the connection is between the design and an elephant's foot.

I just unfolded the photo of you I keep in my wallet, the one I took last winter—your dimples, your pink cheeks, your blonde hair poking out of that orange beanie I love. The corners of the photo are brittle and curve down reminding me of a fitted sheet over the corners of a mattress. Did you know this is the only photo I've made of you? Remember, you had closed your eyes. I was ready when you opened them and snapped. But then you stepped forward and lowered my camera with your hand. No photos of me, you said. And I loved you so much I didn't think I could stand it. If I could choose only one of my photos to keep, this would be it.

I want more photos of you. All the different faces you make that you don't even know you're making, all the different people you can be. That light when you look at me.

I used to feel disconnected when I was here, as if I could disappear without a sound. As if there were no reason to go home. I used to wonder where home was.

I write this, not knowing when you'll read it. Whenever that is, I'll still be thinking of you. This constant craving for you.

All my love, Ethan

Her head fell into her hands. How could this be happening?

She folded the letter and replaced the stack, then opened the drawer above it—photos of Ethan in Afghanistan. In the first, five pairs of his blue and white boxers hang like flags from the pegs of the coat stand in the corner of a room. The washerwoman had refused to wash men's underwear, and there was no running water, so he'd managed it in a bucket. In the next one, Ethan wore a dark gray *shalwar* and *kameez*, a black-and-white scarf, a black *pakol*—with a full beard. When she'd first seen it, she'd barely recognized him, and once she had, it looked like dress-up, but she'd understood in seconds that it was the farthest thing from it. It was the other Ethan—the one she had refused to know.

Cass placed her hand flat against the solid top of the desk. Somehow her great-great-grandmother had known she would need something that would always be beside her.

The phone rang, and she just stared at it. Wheeler came in and picked it up.

Cass left the room. Fear buzzed through her, charging down her arms and legs, which ached with something else, too. She couldn't stay still and began to pace, her steps loud and heavy— up and down the hallway, back and forth, again and again—until she stopped in front of the door to their large guest bathroom, which, except for showers, Ethan used when he was home. This was exactly where she'd stopped in the middle of the night when he'd been on the phone with Setara. She kicked the door open. Bloody hell. To leave her with nothing just when she was supposed to have...She slammed the door shut, locking it.

There was a knock. "You okay, Cass?" Wheeler asked.

She managed a yes and flipped on the light, leaning back against the wall, trying to slow her breath. It felt like a hotel bathroom. No tangy shaving cream on the counter, no brush with black curls spilling out. But there in a basket, untouched, the most recent issue of *People* magazine, waiting for his return, and she slid down the wall. She loved how much he loved *People* magazine. She couldn't bear this.

Across from her on the wall, over the towel rack, one of his photos, one he'd chosen. A man washing burkas and hanging them out to dry. But in the background, two women and a man sitting in the trunk of a yellow car, and in the foreground, three men, each pushing a wheelbarrow full of red pomegranates. So much movement—so unlike the photos she'd chosen for the den.

This man she loved had wanted more than the colorful burkas, and he knew how to wait—she could see it in the photo. He'd been satisfied only when all the differing elements came into play. And this man was the same man who'd made her comfortable in her own skin from the first moment they'd met. Comfortable, and then not, when she began to feel the pull toward what he wanted. And then she had pulled back, as if it were only a matter of sheets.

They'd now been married three years. Phase one of Tidal Flats was over. And she had no idea if they'd ever celebrate this anniversary. May's words. *You think it will be forever, a carpet that will never stop unrolling...*

She stared at the photo, only able to see all that separated them, the continents and that endless gray ocean.

41

Wheeler talked, Cass nodded, her hands upturned in her lap. The embers of last winter's fires still trapped behind glass. It had taken three hours to get the money to Baquir. Then he had to go from Kabul all the way back to Bamiyan. The National Directorate of Security was following behind, but the road was open. It had been four hours since they'd heard anything. She could just make out half a charred log.

"I need some water," Wheeler said. "You need some water. Drink."

In front of her, a cup she lifted to her mouth. Her body would explode if she didn't get off the sofa, but she couldn't move. First, she couldn't stay still, and now she couldn't move. She hadn't moved in hours, more than two. Small vibrations radiated out her arms, one after another, leaving her skin feeling as if she had the flu.

Wheeler let Vee in and Cass stared, imagining him taking Vee in his arms, but he just took the pizza box and shut the door. The smell of garlic and onions and tomatoes reached Cass at the exact moment she wondered if Ethan would ever take her in his arms again, and she had to run for the bathroom, where she gagged into the toilet, her breath stopping, no air getting through, nothing falling out.

Vee pulled her hair from each side of her face.

"I'm okay," Cass said, reclaiming her hair. Somehow she'd become the odd man out. Vee left, shutting the door behind her. Cass locked it.

Something was building inside her. She closed the lid and sat, and the floor spread out in front of her, one tiny white tile leading to another one and another one and another one. For the second time in hours, she found herself in this bathroom. But she didn't want to be out there just fine, unharmed, eating pizza. She didn't want to *watch* anymore. She wanted to be inside it with Ethan, and she wanted to love his Afghanistan. Her hands fell to her thighs, and she felt the bullet and pulled it out of her jeans. She held tight, making wish after promise after wish. She needed to do something and stood and kicked the wall. Ethan was right—she did hate the part of him that loved Afghanistan, and she could see no way to ever loving it.

Vee screamed, and Cass stood and squeezed into the far corner of the bathroom. She wrapped her arms around herself, cradling her elbows in the palms of her hands, the bullet against bone, hardening her body, bracing for the blow.

Banging on the door. Wheeler. "He's free, Cass. You can come out now. He's safe."

42

Late that Atlanta night, early the next Kabul morning, Cass lay in bed, the heavy black phone on her chest. The ambassador had said Ethan would be able to call as soon as he arrived at the embassy, and she was not letting go of this phone until she talked to him.

At the first shudder of a ring—had it even rung—she grabbed the receiver. "Ethan?"

"Cass."

"Ethan," she said again, this time like a breath.

"Are you okay?" he asked.

"Are *you* okay?"

"I am." He cleared his throat a couple of times.

"I don't know how to love someone across an ocean."

"I felt it, though. The whole time they had me."

She struggled not to cry. "Were you scared? I was so scared."

"I was scared, too. I just kept thinking about you. Not you worried but you on the breakwater in Provincetown, your hair blowing around under that cap. I loved you for wanting me to come home each night. I did. I played us like a movie, and if I got a scene out of order, I started at the beginning again. It was your orange beanie, your blue jean jacket, your canvas messenger bag I held onto. God, I miss you, Cass."

As he talked, she squeezed her eyes shut, missing him, missing him, missing him. His voice like an undercurrent. "Did they hurt you?" she asked.

"A few bruises from when they shoved me into the back of the van. Some cuts on my wrists from the rope. Nothing. They left me by myself, tied to a chair in a black room. That was the worst thing—the dark. I couldn't tell up from down. I couldn't see my legs. It was like I only existed in my brain. Like I no longer had a body."

Below the receiver, her right thumb touched the soft spot underneath her left wrist. Chills echoed down her arm.

"Hardly any water, though. My throat feels swollen."

"Where were you when the security forces got there?"

"Baquir and I were in the van. After he delivered the money, they tied him up again. Two of the kidnappers had gone back for Setara. I guess they went out the front. They got away—with her." Cass could hear him take a breath. "They beat her up, Cass. Badly. Her jaw might be broken."

"I'm so sorry, Ethan."

"I know," he said, sounding exhausted.

Despite his painting a different picture, she imagined the two of them together, huddled in a corner, his arm shielding her.

"Wheeler and Vee were here."

"I knew Wheeler would be there," he said. "I'm glad Vee was too."

"Wheeler said they got most of the money back."

"All the cameras are gone."

"I'm sorry, E. I know how much you wanted this."

"I hate it, babe, but I have to get off this phone."

"Not yet," she said. "Please. Just another minute."

"I want to come home, Cass." He started coughing. "But here I might be able to help. The minute Setara's free, I'll be on a plane."

Completely reasonable, she told herself, but she could feel the pressure rising and bit her tongue, adding another notch. She couldn't compete with Afghanistan. "Be safe," she said. "I love you." And then she hung up so she didn't have to hear the click when he did.

She didn't replace the phone on the desk. She kept it on her chest for its weight, for the weight of something.

Neither had mentioned their anniversary. Where he was, that

day had come and gone, and where she was, the word meant too much and not enough. She turned toward the sky that covered both of them but that was still dark over her.

43

Cass knocked on May's door. Hearing no response, she opened it slowly to a dark room.

May lifted her head off the bed. "Cass?"

"It's me."

May wore her gray Bon Iver T-shirt with white waves and windows on it. *Waves into the Soul.* "Ella helped me order it from the Internet," she'd said ages ago. "I just wanted the T-shirt. But the money goes to support the Interval House Women's Shelter in Toronto, which made it even better." Ages ago, that hadn't made Cass think of Vee, but now it did. And for a minute, life felt like a quilt, pieces being added here and there as if there were no plan but in the end a pattern you could see.

"You don't feel good?" Cass said when she stood next to the bed.

May reached for Cass's hand and held it against her chest. Cass wanted to reach up and touch her face, but when May let go, Cass held her hand in front of her face instead. "Can you see my hand?" she asked.

"I can see your pretty nails."

"You can't read my palms?"

"The Madame cannot see your palms. But don't despair. She can feel your aura."

"How's my aura doing?"

"Your aura is sad, and I don't need any special talent to know that."

"Let's get you some sunshine."

"You mean, let's get *us* some sunshine," May said.

"You love the rays coming in." Cass turned from raising the

shade to May.

"Ella told me your Ethan was kidnapped but that he's safe now. So why are you sad?"

Cass sank into May's favorite chair. "He's not coming home yet, and he was supposed to be home for good by now."

"Oh, Cass," she said.

"It's time for him to come home."

"If he's not coming home to you, he must really need to be there."

Which made Cass pause.

"What if when you died you became a character in someone's book?" May asked. "I was just thinking about that before you came in. Or a figure in someone's painting? Wouldn't that be lovely?"

"It would," Cass said.

She should file a report and call the nurse, but the nurse would be here later anyway. Cass scooted closer and opened the book. But instead of starting to read, again she looked at May. She said her name, and May opened her eyes. "I was wondering about your heart, how you used it up."

May smiled. "I started early, by loving a boy who didn't love me back." She spoke word by word. Enunciating. "I told everyone I loved him. But this was high school." She paused, swallowed. "My girlfriends accused me of having no pride. When people think of heart, they think of love. When I think of heart, I think of feeling— something, anything, everything. And I always felt it—whatever it was." She opened her arms wide but started coughing and brought her hands in to cover her mouth.

Cass put the book down and helped May sit up straighter, held the glass of water for her, got her settled again.

"All those feelings," May whispered. "It's like...like riding in a truck on a bumpy road. You can brace yourself with your hands and feet, steel your body against the bumps, and try to have a smooth ride. Or you can let your body go and roll all around." She relaxed back against the pillow. "I wanted to feel every bump."

But Cass had been steeling herself for as long as she could remember—trying to hold steady, pushing back, protecting. Saving her heart, like she used to do with clothes, waiting to wear each new shirt on a date before wearing it to school. She'd forgotten about that self. The high school self without a care in the world, except for a weird mother and everybody's mother was weird. But what was she saving her heart for now?

May's eyes were closed again.

"Top of page forty-six," Cass said. May always wanted to know the page numbers.

Mick sat on the steps a long time. Miss Brown did not turn on her radio and there was nothing but the noises that people made. She thought a long time and kept hitting her thighs with her fists. Her face felt like it was scattered in pieces and she could not keep it straight. The feeling was a whole lot worse than being hungry for any dinner, yet it was like that. I want—I want—I want—was all that she could think about—but just what this real want was she did not know.

44

The next day, as light left the sky, the landline rang.

"Setara's dead."

Two words. That was it. As if it were her fault.

"Ethan," she whispered, dropping into her chair. "I'm so sorry."

"And now the police won't release her body."

"What happened?"

"They left her. Outside RAWA headquarters. She was beaten to death."

"Oh, no, Ethan." She leaned over, her elbows on her legs, her head falling into her hand. "I thought she would come through this. She's always seemed so tough. I can't believe it." But his clipped sentences hung in the air. They leaked something she couldn't figure out. Or contained something. Something other than sadness. "What about you? Are you in danger, too?"

"I'm fine."

Did he think she had wanted this? Hadn't she? No, she had not wanted this.

"Are you leaving today?"

"I have to go down to the police station," he said.

"Tomorrow?" Like a child, she wanted him to come home.

"There may be other issues," he said, clearing his throat. "I can't leave yet."

He didn't come home after he was rescued. He wasn't coming home now. Maybe he was never coming home.

"Are you there?" he asked.

"I'm sorry Setara's dead." She sat back up. "And I'm sorry for her husband and her baby. And I'm sorry for you, Ethan. But what about us?"

"I'll be home as soon as I can. There are issues. Because of Setara's death. It's complicated."

"I miss you," she said. "And I'm worried about you. But all these phone calls telling me you're not coming home? If you don't want to come home, just say it."

And then there was silence. No static or breathing but silence. She hadn't meant to say it, but she'd taken her foot off the brake, and it had come out of her mouth.

"I *am* coming home, Cass. I want to be there now. Can you hold on a little longer? Tidal Flats, remember?"

She was about to tell him he'd broken Tidal Flats when he spoke again.

"I'm sorry, Cass. I..." His voice shook.

And she held her breath.

After a while, she said, "Are you okay, E?"

"I know you're tired of this, Cass," he said. "*I'm* tired of it. I love you more than anything."

She listened to all the miles between them, told him she loved him, too, and hung up, unsure of what to grab for that wouldn't sink her faster.

45

As usual, Cass sat in the light-filled atrium drinking coffee while she waited for the text from Ethan that he was finished at customs. This time felt different, though. It had been three long weeks since the night he'd called to tell her about Setara's death and she'd asked him to come home, and there'd been other difficult phone calls just like that one. Now, after all these years, he was coming home for good, and yet it wasn't the way she'd imagined it. She was excited, yes, but there was something else in the air—some uncertainty or sadness or unsaid thing between them. Or maybe it had just cost too much.

On her computer, the GoFundMe page showed the account up to $48,264 raised by 542 people. At the top corner of her computer, the time confirmed customs *was* taking longer than it normally did. Her foot tapped and her stomach felt turbulent. She opened her email and reread the message she'd gotten from him yesterday.

On the way home. Will you pick me up tomorrow morning like usual? Love, Ethan.

That was all he wrote. Over the years, that was often all he wrote.

Around her, people in transit or people waiting for those who were. Despite the large area, sound was muted and soft.

And then there was his text. *Done.*

She flicked her phone to silent. One last sip of coffee, a drink out of her water bottle, computer unplugged, and messenger bag across her body. She picked up the white roses she'd brought for him but held them to her side.

As she made her way from the tall, airy space through the hallway to the flat, boxy area in front of the escalators, one end of which opened into the South Terminal, the other into the North, her calmness disappeared, and in its stead, low-rolling jolts of her heart. As she merged into the waiting crowd that was roped against the far wall, the noise slammed into her. Groups pulled together, leaving gaps for her to wind her way to the front. All these people facing forward, all the attention focused on the escalators on the other side of the wide canyon where the arriving passengers would appear.

Soldiers in camouflage rose up and peeled off to the South Terminal. A woman sneezed. Someone coughed. A child lay down on the floor beside her feet. When she looked back up, Ethan's black curls. And the beard, again. And then someone else's black curls. In one hand hanging down by his side, Ethan held a black bag she'd never seen before. In the other, raised up to the level of his waist, Ethan was holding a baby.

Cass glanced to the left and the right. Families on both sides of her. Facing forward again, it *was* Ethan. And it *was* a baby. And those eyes. Coming toward her.

She took a step back but landed on someone's shoes, losing her balance for a second. Pinpricks zipped down her body. Ethan and the eyes were so close now. The pinpricks raced up into her neck, into her face. Perhaps her body was trying to cut off oxygen to her brain. Too late.

This dark man who stood in front of her with a thorny beard seemed foreign, unfamiliar, dangerous.

"This is Amala," he said, his soft voice shocking her.

"I know who it is," she said, her harsh voice shocking her. "Why is she with you?" Her words felt like shards. She felt out of control, wild. Why hadn't she busted into pieces?

He took a step back. His eyes were wide. Or was it her eyes?

"Cass, let's...go somewhere to talk."

"Why do you have Setara's baby?"

But as she asked the question, she looked from Ethan to the

baby, who stared at her with the same expression as Ethan—neither one smiling—and in the second before he said it, she knew the answer and covered her ears, but she heard the words anyway.

○ ○ ○

Cass felt her heart cramping and shrinking, pulling away from the surrounding tissue, forming a hollow gutter around itself, and then there was its weight—too heavy and bearing down on the rest of her. She couldn't breathe. She couldn't speak. Time stopped. She froze it, refusing to go forward beyond that moment. There was nothing on the other side. Nothing to hold her up. She would be falling forever.

She willed herself to lose consciousness, and at the same time not to, not to cede her body to anyone for no one could be trusted. There were no words. And yet she had one. *Away.*

Away from all these people who were waiting for someone they knew. Away from the escalators that continued to spit out travelers. Away from this area that had only two exits. Away from this world where nothing was ever the way it was supposed to be. Away from the man she had married. Away from the child in his arms.

Where she was supposed to be.

Away was where she was going and when she came to a huge expanse of blank wall, she dropped her head against its numbing coldness. She closed her eyes. The hard, unforgiving wall made sense. This was her world. But then the wall changed shape. Like a dry, empty river basin at a sudden rain fills with water. And the harder she tried to reach the other side, the surer she was that she would drown—swirling, caught up in a current, being swept out to sea.

It was her fault. She hadn't stopped him. If only she could have prevented the words from leaving his mouth. She had failed to react in time. Again.

She lifted one foot and let it fall. And she did that again and again. And when she had taken herself away, her chest heaved out a breath. She could walk. And she just kept walking. Into the crowds of passengers and people waiting for passengers, into stores, into the backs of airport restaurants and out again. She waited in the long and winding security line, moving inch by inch until she made it to the front and then returning to the end to get in line again. She joined the masses of passengers wanting tickets away from here. Finally, she gravitated to baggage claim, moving in close to the ones who were left empty-handed as the carousel stopped and the light went out.

46

Only when it was dark outside did she feel it was safe to leave the airport. As she approached the glass doors, they opened and she walked into a rectangular cubicle, the transition area—not inside and not outside. Too fast, the second set of glass doors parted, and she could hear the horns and the door slams, the policeman's whistle. She could see the flashing blue light and taste the gasoline-laced exhaust of cars idling in park several layers deep out from the curb. Up ahead, the even darker parking garage, concentrated darkness waiting for her. She picked up speed. When she reached for the door handle, the cold, slick metal snapped back and she lost her balance again. Inside the car, she closed the door, but threw it open and leaned over, gagging on the emptiness. This time when the door shut, she felt safe, but her arm was too heavy to lift the key, too heavy for sure to hold the wheel long enough to get her back to town.

How dry her throat was. Her water bottle was still in her purse, which surprised her, but this one small action in favor of herself—reaching into her purse for water—encouraged her. She reached again—to turn the key in the ignition. But as she examined her two hands on the steering wheel, she remembered the roses, and she didn't know what had happened to them.

Go now, she told herself. *Put the car in reverse, put your life in reverse.* She was looking behind her, not relying on mirrors. She went back and back and back until her bumper grazed the bumper of another car. Then she put the car in drive, and she drove, the route from the airport to what she used to call home as familiar and as strange as the man she'd encountered inside.

o ○ o

Finding herself in the apartment's underground parking garage, she parked. But she couldn't turn the car off, couldn't get out. Reverse again. And she took herself away, feeling her confidence grow. Reverse, reverse, reverse. Hunger. Down Howell Mill, a Waffle House. Again, she couldn't get out of the car. Eggs and bacon had always been their first meal. She clinched and unclenched her fingers. Behind her, as she backed up, a strip mall and a Mexican restaurant. Inside, she ordered rice and beans. And water.

Heading back to the car after eating, she ran her hand through the darkness in front of her and felt no resistance, only a breeze cool on her skin. In the car, she faced the steering wheel without hesitation. She would be fine, she told herself. She just needed to regroup, get a different plan for her life. Two doors down was a liquor store, and she bought a six-pack of Blue Moon. She passed her apartment without looking at it, and three blocks later, found a little hole-in-the-wall hotel she'd never noticed before.

She parked on the street. Her messenger bag purse was still across her body where she'd let it stay through dinner like a seat belt. She hadn't thought of her phone since morning—before. She found it in her purse. Thirty-three missed calls from Ethan. A *New York Times* update. Voicemails she didn't listen to. Texts she didn't read. In the backseat, she found a bag she used for groceries and dropped in a hairbrush and lotion from the glove compartment. She found a book long forgotten and added that. Tomorrow she would face the apartment, retrieve clean clothes, more books. After that, there would be work. And May to read to. And Atta and Lois. And Vee and Singer. She surveyed the dark, empty car, then got out, beeped to lock it, and headed inside to book a room. *How many nights?* she imagined the clerk asking. *The rest of them*, she would say.

47

The hotel bed was unfamiliar, but it was supposed to be. Cass drew her body in, smaller and smaller, but she couldn't stop her brain—now showing videos of Ethan rising on the escalator, Ethan and a baby in the apartment that used to belong to the two of them. Now showing videos of Ethan and Setara.

She needed something to push against and dropped her feet to the hotel floor. She needed something to slow her brain that was dismantling the only good and solid life she'd ever known as if it had been a set on a stage temporarily erected. *The show had had a good long run. Some considered it a success. Closing was always sad.* The library, she imagined that's where she was going. Just a normal Saturday. Think of all the books.

When she stepped out of the hotel and onto the sidewalk, it was oppressive. Humid and hot. And not quite June yet. She raised her arm against the light and retreated into the shadow of the awning. Digging for sunglasses, she thought of the nearby jail that worried Ethan and wished she were headed there. She would interview the prisoners. *What was it like,* she would ask, *to have the life you'd known taken away from you?* And the ones being released—she imagined them hanging around, not being able to move forward, looking longingly back at the bars.

Off you go, she told herself, after a man in a suit stepped around her, his black-loafered feet pointing away from each other, his briefcase hanging down by his side as if it wanted to collapse onto the pavement.

Up ahead, on the other side of the street in what she thought was normally a vacant lot, was a mini carnival. She could see balloons, a merry-go-round, a death-trap of a roller coaster, a multicolored tent, and a circular enclosure that had to be that scary ride that spun you around until you stuck to the side—where you had to trust something you couldn't see and that made no sense, and then to prove it, to prove that you *could* trust something you couldn't see, the floor dropped away, taking your insides with it.

In the block ahead on the right were the Fates, who didn't expect her until day four. She brushed against the edgy metal of a street sign and pushed her hand against her stomach. Everything was too full, claustrophobic, too many different colors of green.

In the next block, the construction site—the building almost finished and yet so far from being habitable. On the other side of the street, their apartment. *His. His apartment.* As she waited for the light to change, she heard the roar of not one but many motorcycles and the pumping of accelerators. She didn't have to look to see hands rolling forward, revving motors, as they paused for the light. She wouldn't look.

When the light changed, she stepped into the crosswalk at the same time that hundreds of motorcycles sped forward. Too loud. She covered her ears and jumped back. As she listened to the noise fade into the distance, she inched toward the building where she'd lived for the last three years of her life. She faced the door and reached for the knob.

48

It seemed as if she should knock, but she wouldn't ask permission. Inside, the sun barged through the windows but was no match for the dark, soundless apartment. Suitcases littered the den floor. Dirty dishes and a bottle sat on the coffee table. She wasn't trying to be quiet, but she didn't seem able to make any noise.

The door to the guest bathroom was closed; the door to the bedroom, open. An overcast day was what she would have ordered if she'd thought to. Gray and sad.

Ethan, asleep on the bed.

She was not sneaking in. She was coming to claim what was hers. In her closet, she pulled out the step stool to retrieve her suitcase. As she touched the handle of the tapestry bag she'd packed and unpacked so many times she'd lost count before she even got to high school, ripples traveled through her body. No longer was there anyone to keep up with. There was just her. She pulled with more strength than necessary but recovered, swung the suitcase to the floor, and stepped off the stool. Underwear, shorts, shirts, running shoes, her jean jacket. This was a temporary solution. For permanent, she would have to come back with boxes.

He stirred.

For a second, she froze, and then she proceeded to her desk. Into her leather backpack went her phone charger, and notepads. She turned her wedding photo facedown. A handful of pencils and pens and books—

"Cass?"

As if someone had reached inside her, grabbed her heart, and yanked. She rubbed her chest. May Sarton and Rumi—

And then he was beside her, and he reached for her arm.

"Don't touch me," she said, not looking at him.

He dropped his arm. "Can we talk?"

She returned to her closet for the bottle of Xanax. When she came out, she gave him a wide berth, making sure nothing got between her and the door. "It's over."

"Cass," he said, drawing out her name. He had no right to do that.

"Don't say my name," she said, too loud. But she wanted him to ask her to be quiet because the baby was sleeping. Where, she didn't know, but she wanted to see what she would do then. *Just tell me to be quiet. Just try that.*

"Can we sit down?"

She raised the handle on her suitcase, slung her backpack over her shoulder, and left the bedroom.

"Don't just leave," he said.

She concentrated on making it through the narrow hallway, past the kitchen.

"Please don't go," he said. "Let me explain."

As she passed the back-to-back sofas, she saw them—Cass and Ethan—sitting on the breakwater in the middle of the tidal flats. And she stopped. Something rose up in her throat, and she couldn't swallow. That day the water had swirled around them, splashing onto them. They hadn't been able to see what lay beneath the surface. But now it was almost low tide, and she could see everything—the particles of sand, the ripple marks, the abandoned shells, the small mounds, the tiny air holes, the debris. If she could just hear the foghorn. But it was quiet. Behind her, Ethan stood, watching her. Ahead of her, the front door seemed too far away and as if the knob were already in her hand. *Turn it*, she told herself. *Grab hold and turn.* But she wasn't moving. She turned back to Ethan. "You had sex with Setara?"

She hadn't intended to say anything, much less that, something beyond obvious. She hadn't intended to say *her* name. She hadn't intended for her voice to go up at the end of those words but her body—hoping against clear evidence—betrayed her. She'd lost control of herself.

Ethan looked afraid. She wasn't sure she'd ever seen him afraid.

That day so long ago when they'd sat back to back in the middle of the water, she hadn't been able to see his face. But now she looked straight at him. She saw his dark eyes, his beard.

"Yes," he whispered, into the quiet in which they stood, but the word picked up volume and heft on its trajectory and slammed into her.

"Say the whole thing," she said, tightening her grip on the suitcase handle. Her eyes found the fireplace full of embers, the French doors sharply lit, the blank TV, the large green leaves of the plant dropping closer and closer to the floor.

"I had sex with Setara."

And the water paused for a moment, as if it were surprised, too.

Her eyes filled with tears. She could trust no one. Not her mother to take care of her or her father not to die.

"This whole time you've been having sex with Setara?" She ran out of breath at the end of the question and inhaled for more. Her hand widened and wrapped around the handle of the suitcase, its ridges pressing into her palm. She let go for a minute to see what would happen. Nothing. She was still here and still standing.

"No, Cass," he said. "One time."

She looked at him again. Puffiness and fatigue clouded his face, greasy hair sticking every which way, dark circles under his eyes, something red spilled down his blue T-shirt, his pajama pants dragging the floor.

"I didn't love Setara," he said. "I never wanted a life with her. I never wanted a child with her."

A child. Leave now. Why wasn't she leaving? She cleared her throat and adjusted her backpack on her shoulder. "All these months." She grabbed her stomach. "You didn't tell me even after she got pregnant?"

"I didn't know. She didn't tell me anything. It was one time, Cass."

"I told you not to say my name."

"There were bombs going off all around us, and we got separated from the others. We thought we were safe, but then a bomb blew the back off the shack where we were, and we were trapped. We thought we were going to die. It was the middle of the night in the middle of nowhere. Hours and hours, all night long, facedown in the dirt and fighting all around us. We were two human beings together in the darkness, holding on to each other for the seconds we had left in the world. That's not an excuse. It happened. But it didn't happen because I loved her. It was fear and circumstances. I hated myself afterward. And I knew how I'd hurt you. It was one time. One mistake."

Dead low tide.

Way out there, in a place she couldn't see, the water reversed course, and the waves crashed against each other. Cass felt dizzy, and her eyes blurred. She pulled her suitcase closer. There was a rushing in her ears, and she found the doorknob and opened the door, but she turned back to Ethan. "You thought you were going to die, and you never told me?"

49

In her hotel room, she kept hold of her suitcase. What day was it? Was she supposed to be at work? Ethan had arrived on a Friday. She had come here. Was that only yesterday? The longer she stood still, the closer she felt she was getting to the floor. She would walk. That's what she would do. She would pound it all away.

Once outside, she wanted something that was supposed to be unfamiliar.

The Fulton County Jail. It took up a whole block. And there were guards and rolls and rolls of barbed wire. She walked around its four sides again and again and again, becoming aware, at some point, of a tender spot on her right heel. By the time she got to the library, she was sweating, and the nail of one of her toes was slicing into the toe next to it. Inside, she leaned against a shelf, resting her head on the books, letting the air conditioning wash over her.

"Why aren't you with Ethan?" Vee said.

Cass jumped.

"I didn't mean to scare you."

Cass opened her mouth but couldn't say anything. She should never have come here and turned away from Vee.

"What's the matter, Cass?" Vee said. "You look terrible."

Still nothing came out of her mouth.

Vee grabbed hold of her arm and led her through the stacks to the back wall next to a door marked *Emergency Exit*. She pulled her to the floor between two shelves, close and contained. With Vee's hand still on her arm and when she didn't let go, Cass said, "Ethan brought Setara's baby home, only it's his baby, too."

"No fucking way," Vee said, her eyes narrowing.

Cass rocked back and forth. It was all real now.

"I can't believe it."

"I just left them at the airport. I left them there."

"Of course you did." Vee leaned forward and wrapped her arms around Cass.

"I went to a hotel."

"I wish you'd called me." Vee sat back.

"I couldn't think, I couldn't breathe, I couldn't make it make sense. It felt...impossible."

Vee kept shaking her head, which felt right to Cass.

"How old's the baby?"

"I don't know. Little. Born in January."

"Four months," Vee said. "Shit."

"Ethan had sex with Setara. Setara was killed. He brought her baby home. His baby."

"I can't believe Ethan would do that. What does he say?"

"I can't talk to him."

"He's still Ethan."

"I don't know that he is. And I don't know that he has been for a while."

Vee straightened her legs out in front of her, and so did Cass.

"When I saw her in that towel in his room, and he said it was nothing, that her shower was broken, I believed him. I'm so stupid." She didn't want to cry, but she couldn't help it.

"Fuck," Vee said. "I thought he was one of the good ones."

"I have to keep my phone turned off. I don't want to hear his voice, see his name—"

"But you're going to have to talk to him sometime."

"I want my stuff out of there. I want my desk."

"Oh, Cass."

She dropped her head into her hands.

"Maybe the baby's not his?" Vee said. "Maybe she made the whole thing up."

Cass raised her head. "That would solve one problem. But he

still slept with her. He told me. And the baby looks like him. They have the same black curls."

"But Setara had black hair, too."

"The baby has her eyes."

"You need to talk to him."

"Not with that baby around."

"What if I keep the baby and Ethan meets you somewhere? Could you talk to him if it were Ethan by himself?"

"Maybe." But Cass felt pressure on her chest, as if she were deep under water.

"I'll call Wheeler," Vee said. "I'll get him to call Ethan. We'll set it up for tomorrow evening."

Bookshelves towered almost to the ceiling. There was the emergency exit.

"Come on," Vee said again, standing and pulling Cass to her feet. "It wasn't a question."

"I don't want to know details. Just tell him to meet me... where?" She grabbed a shelf. "Where can we meet?"

"The bar?"

"No."

"Right."

Cass rubbed her chest again. For the first time since Ethan had gotten home, she remembered Singer in their apartment and the kiss. And for a second, she understood how it could have happened and meant nothing other than circumstances.

"The bar at the hotel where I'm staying," she said. "The Rose House. A few blocks from here. Tell him to meet me there. *If* he wants to talk."

50

At six thirty, Cass sat down on the booth side of a table in the back of the quiet hotel bar. She'd come down early, so she could choose a spot where she could see the entrance and so she wouldn't be the one looking for him.

Several hours ago, she'd called Vee to cancel, saying she didn't have anything to say, no place even to start. "Let the burden be on him," Vee had said. "He'll be there at seven." When Cass had stopped trying to figure out what she would say, she'd stopped feeling like she was going to jump out of her skin. She'd been able to breathe. Vee was right, she'd decided. Let him be the one to start.

Now, though, her stomach was uneasy again, and she took a mouthful of wine. It was a small bar—just a counter and an alcove with a few tables. The only other person there was a woman on a bar stool, working on a computer. The candles on the tables flickered as the outside door, across the lobby, opened from time to time. Green was the only decorating theme Cass could discern. She shook out her arms, rolled her shoulders back. Six fifty-three by her phone. And there he was.

Without his beard.

He stepped in, wiping his hands on his pants. He had put on a sport coat.

But his eyes landing on her felt sudden and loud, making her want to throw her hands up in front of her face. And yet she couldn't take her eyes off him. She felt a knot in her chest. Then he was standing there, reaching a hand out toward her arm. She didn't move, wasn't sure she could have if she'd tried. She never actually felt him touch her. Perhaps he had and she just hadn't felt it. He sat across from her.

It was as if she hadn't seen him in years, as if time had fast-forwarded to a place where they were now looking back on different lives the other one knew nothing about. Sadness began to move through her like anesthesia. Perhaps later, she wouldn't remember what was about to happen now.

The waitress took his order and brought him a drink—a short glass, tawny liquid, ice.

Burgundy liquid in her own glass, which she turned in circle after circle.

His glass thudded back to the table, the ice cubes clanking. He stood, sat down next to her, and wrapped his arms around her, but her arms hung limp. Breath after breath, the rise and fall of his chest. It was so familiar that, without permission, her arms responded.

"I'm so sorry, Cass," he whispered. "I messed everything up. This is not what I wanted."

Her head found his shoulder.

"I'm so sorry, babe," he said.

She lifted her head, separated herself, and locked her hands around her glass. "You can't call me that anymore."

"I don't want a life without you," he said, then reached across the table for his glass and finished off the drink. "But I can't abandon the baby."

She felt the anesthesia wearing off, the sadness slipping away. And a new thread or one she had missed. "Your child, you mean." She spit the words out.

"My child."

She wanted to smash something. "How do you know she's even yours?"

Ethan reached into his jacket pocket and pulled out an envelope, which he placed on the table in front of her. "Paternity test," he said. "Everything takes so long over there. But I didn't want to...I couldn't come back before I knew for sure."

She stared at the white envelope that there was no need to

open, feeling a blanket of weights descend upon her.

"I'm such an idiot," she said. "For believing you when you said there was nothing between you and her."

"You're not an idiot. I am. I'm the one who messed up. But it was just one time, Cass. One time."

"What difference does that make?"

"I didn't love her. I didn't have a relationship with her. It was one night."

He was trying to straighten a more wrinkled envelope against the hard surface of the table. This second envelope had his name on it in cursive—large, thin black letters.

"I didn't know the baby was mine until after Setara was dead and Feda gave me the letter. Still, I didn't believe it. I thought Setara just wanted her child to have a different life and that she was using me to make it happen. So I had the paternity test done."

He should have given her the letter first, then the paternity test. It was the wrong order.

Cass looked at him and then away, fixing her eyes on the woman at the bar. Feda. Setara's husband in name only, no different than her burka. Allowing her to travel the streets unnoticed. In search of freedom. In search of what she wanted.

She looked back at Ethan.

His gaze didn't waver.

This time neither did hers. "Who are you?"

"The same person. The person who loves you."

"You're not."

"I am."

She looked away again.

He pushed the letter toward her. "Will you read it? Please."

She didn't want to take what he was offering. She wanted what was in the spidery envelope not to matter. But she picked it up. And she opened it. The letter was on pale white paper, thin and unlined. The same black ink, the same thin cursive.

Dear Ethan,

If all had gone according to plan, you would never have known. But if you're reading this letter, something has happened to me, and you must take responsibility for Amala. She is our hope. She is the future. She is yours.

As much as I love this country and struggled for it to be a place where Amala, and all children who were born here, could grow up in peace and full potential, my Afghanistan is not ready yet. Take Amala home with you.

Teach her to love this country the way you do, the way you look past the struggle at the beauty, the way you find the hearts and souls of our people, the way you found me.

I hope you do not hate me for that night, for making your love of this country human, for turning your love into hope. If you do, it is a necessary thing. Please do not hold it against our daughter.

For hope,

S

Shivers from her chest to her elbows to her legs. Shivers across her teeth. She didn't look at him. She couldn't. The letter fell to the table as she left.

51

Routine. On her way to work, she stopped by the coffee shop. The usual? the girl asked. Cass nodded. A medium latte with coconut milk. Like always.

But when she collected her coffee and turned to leave, she could feel the blister on her heel from the endless walking and how her body ached. She'd been holding herself too tight—clinching to brace and contain herself. When the bell rang as she opened the café door, she stopped where she was. It was all true. There were no more maybes.

She couldn't go forward and moved to the side, out of the way, stopping inches before leaning against the building. It was the same place she'd stood with the brick at her back and the sky in front of her after she'd seen Setara in Ethan's room. That day, she'd listened to his voice telling her that nothing was going on. She had believed him. But what he hadn't told her was that the damage had already been done.

The wrought iron table. She sat, lifted her head to the warm sun, and closed her eyes. As she drank her coffee, she thought of May and Atta and Lois. When she stood, she paused over the trash can. Only a few sips of cold coffee stared at her from the bottom of her cup, but she couldn't throw it away.

$$\circ \, {}^{\circ} \circ$$

When Cass opened Howell's front door, Atta was sitting on the sofa in the foyer holding a lemon and a pair of scissors. "I was waiting for you," she said. "You're late you know. And I thought, maybe I'll just snip the end off this lemon. Now you can really smell it. And it smells just like a lemon should."

"Why are you waiting for me?" Cass asked. "Is something wrong? Is May worse?"

Atta shook her head. "Nothing's wrong. May's still in bed holding court, but no worse."

"Good," Cass said, relieved.

"*You* don't look good," Atta said, patting the space beside her. "Come sit with me."

Cass knew what she must look like—dirty hair, slept-in clothes. She was turning into her mother, and she didn't have the energy to care. Perhaps that's what made the difference in a life—energy. But she sat next to Atta, still holding on to the empty coffee cup and dropping her bag beside her.

"What's wrong?" Atta asked. "Didn't Ethan get back?"

"He had sex with someone else."

"Damnation," Atta said, slapping her thigh.

"I shouldn't have said that to you. It's inappropriate and unprofessional."

"Child, we are a family. Appropriate and professional can stay on the other side of that door." Atta put the scissors on the table, the lemon back in the bowl, and threw her arms around Cass, holding on for a good minute before she let go. "How bad is it?"

"It was just one time, but there's a baby."

"Lord Jesus. Did he come back?"

"He did. The mother was killed. So now he has the baby."

Atta was patting her back. "I know it doesn't seem like it," she said, "but it's going to be okay."

"My mother wanted to be an artist," Cass said. "I've never been enough for anyone." Tears leaked out of her eyes, and she wiped them away.

"I'm going to tell you a story. When I was a senior in high school, I decided I didn't need anyone but myself. And I lived my life to prove it to everybody."

Cass placed the empty cup on the table in front of her and removed the scarred lemon from the bowl.

"The problem was," Atta said, "*I* was the only one I needed to prove it to." Atta placed her hand on Cass's leg. "The only thing that keeps us from being enough is the fear of not being enough. Know you are enough. Each one of us is. We are each a wonderful little container of enough. Look at me."

Cass did.

"You are enough, Mary Cassatt Miller. Say it."

Cass touched the tender white spot on the lemon and then held it under her nose. Of course, the scent was stronger this way. "I am enough."

"Again, like you mean it."

"I am enough." And she returned the scarred lemon to the bowl.

"Yes, you are. Now you don't have to waste your life on that. You can move from a different place."

Cass sat a little straighter.

Atta sat a little straighter.

"We have a visitor," Atta said. "Remember that teenager from the fundraiser? The Georgia State student?"

"The one you sent to give his change to Ella?"

"That's the one. Turns out he has a mother and that he actually talks to his mother, and she's waiting for you in the kitchen."

Cass stood. "This whole time? In the kitchen? What about our living room with the pretty sofas?"

"That's not us. She wanted something real, I could tell. Fanny fixed tea. She's back there with Lois and Ella."

Leaving Atta on the sofa, Cass took off down the hall. But no one was in the kitchen, so she pushed open the door to the breakfast room. The woman had her back to Cass and stood. She was tall like Vee. Except her hair was not black but blonde like Cass's. She was maybe in her fifties. Black pants, white shirt, and silver everywhere.

"You must be Cass," she said, extending her hand, her bracelets jangling like a wind chime. "I'm Jana Thomas."

Cass shook her hand. "So nice to meet you." Take away the years of unhappiness and depression and Jana Thomas could have been her mother. "Sorry I was late."

"I'm glad you were. Lois has been showing me her iPhone and iPad and photos of graduations and weddings and births, and some selfies of her in her red room."

Cass smiled—and she'd been afraid she'd never smile again.

On the table, a pot of tea and a pitcher of lemonade. Cass looked at the faces—Ella's young, Fanny's light brown, Lois's wrinkled, Jana Thomas's familiar. She'd never met anyone who reminded her of her mother.

"Ladies, it was lovely to meet each of you," Ms. Thomas said. "Perhaps I could come back to visit?"

"Please do," Lois said. "Next time, I might just put on those red heels."

"I'd like that." And then Ms. Thomas turned to Cass, who led her past Atta, standing in the hallway. Ms. Thomas gave Atta a hug. "Thanks for taking me upstairs to meet May."

"Well, I didn't want you to miss anything," Atta said. "She's kind of the main attraction around here."

In the office, Ms. Thomas went straight to the window facing the front courtyard. "This is a special place, Cass."

"I think so too, Ms—"

"Oh, you have to call me Jana. I love the way it feels to be here. Like being part of a family in a home. How did you make it feel like this?"

"I didn't. I was just a volunteer. I fell in love with it, too."

"Real lemons, Atta said."

"I can't handle fake fruit. I bought the first ones with my own money. They didn't think it would make a difference."

"And the iPhones and iPads were your idea, too?" Jana sat down.

"It makes so much sense to me," Cass said, sitting beside her instead of behind her desk. "It's using the brain, it's how people stay in touch these days, it's being a part of the world."

"You're so young...How do you decide who gets to live here? I imagine you have more requests than rooms."

Cass nodded. "There's a waiting list. Each woman who lives here must be self-sufficient and able to follow rules. There's an application. And then an interview. This is assisted living but only in the broadest sense."

"They love you."

"I love them," Cass said.

"My son told me you need money."

"Quite a bit, I'm afraid."

Jana looked toward the foyer. "If you don't live with love, it's all you think about. If you have it, it's so easy to think you don't need it. My husband died ten years ago. My son is in college. I miss being part of a family." She turned to Cass. "How much exactly?"

Cass went back to her desk. She clicked over to the GoFundMe site, signed in, and subtracted what had come in through the mail. "Four hundred forty-nine thousand three hundred fifty dollars."

"Okay," she said, placing her hands on her thighs. "I think I can help." She stood. "May I come back?"

"We'd love to have you."

Jana smiled and headed toward the front door. When she reached for the doorknob, she turned around to Cass. "This may have been a special place before you came or it might have been you who made it this way, your ability to see what it could become. Either way, it's special now. And Atta, Lois, Ella—they think you're pretty special. I hope you won't underestimate what you have to offer, the change you can make in the world. From where I stand, it's quite remarkable." And she stepped toward Cass and gave her a hug.

Cass felt the swell of tears but swallowed them back. Before Jana got in her car, she turned to Cass again and grinned. "I never used to be a hugger." And then she was gone.

52

Cass climbed the steps to her third-floor hotel room. She'd lived by herself before. She could do it again. Maybe she should move back to her old neighborhood. But her mother had always gone backward. Her father had gone forward.

In her room, she sat in the desk chair and opened her computer. She typed in *Atlanta rentals*, clicked on VRBO, but then she had to fill in dates and that stopped her. And next to the dates, the number of guests. She closed her computer and wrapped her arms around herself. A whole apartment would be too much space anyway. What did she want?

She knew what she didn't want—to leave somewhere else. If she couldn't go forward yet, she wanted to stay. To hold steady.

She looked around this room that felt safe. Bed, night table, mini-fridge, microwave, sitting area, TV, desk and chair. No room for anything else. No empty space to fill.

○ ○ ○

Downstairs at the front desk, she asked the guy if there were options.

"We rent by the day, the week, or the month," he said, looking over his glasses and giving her his full attention. "The longer you commit to, the better the rate. Lots of lawyers stay here when they're in trial."

She thought the last bit was supposed to encourage her. "What have I been until now?"

"I was wondering when you were going to ask."

"I've been a little distracted," she said, spotting his nametag.

"I haven't noticed at all," Henry said, smiling and pushing his glasses back up as he looked at the computer. "You've been day to day, I'm afraid." He raised his eyebrows. "If you opt for a longer stay, I can maybe help you out with that."

"Thank you," she said. "I'd like to stay longer."

"Fabulous. We'd love to have you. Week to week, month to month...?"

"A month," she said, handing over her credit card, feeling as if she were, in fact, enough.

"We have everything you need here, don't we? I try to make sure we do. *And* included with the month-long stays is a pass for the exercise studio a couple of doors down. It's called Core. Ask for Finn. You'll love him."

$$\circ \; {}^{\circ} \circ$$

When Cass got back upstairs, her room felt different, more hers. She took the rest of her things out of her suitcase and calculated how much more she could bring over. Maybe she could move her desk to Howell. She wanted to get her things from Ethan's, but at the same time, she didn't. She wondered if she could be content with what she had.

53

This time, she was late on purpose, wanting Ethan to have to wait for her. When she entered the bar, there he was—sitting right where she'd left him three nights ago.

He stood as she slid into the booth side, a glass of wine in front of her place. "What's this?" she asked.

"I ordered you a merlot." His hair was too long. His eyes, puffy. Cass motioned to the waitress. "I'll have a Blue Moon, please," she said. And she pushed the wine to the side, focusing on the people in the bar—more than last time. The waitress delivered her beer, with an orange slice, which she knocked into the glass without squeezing. The carbonation and light rich taste encouraged her, but she had nothing to say. It was up to him. Five minutes, and then she was gone.

"This isn't the way I wanted it to be," he said.

She placed her hand flat on the hard table.

"We can get through this. If you'll come home. We can still be who we were."

"That's impossible," she said, in a whisper.

Ethan leaned forward. "We can be a family, Cass."

"I never wanted a family, Ethan." But the word *family* meant something different to her now. It conjured May and Atta and Lois. "That's not true," she said. "You and I were a family. And I wanted that." She couldn't bear it and started to stand.

He touched her arm, and she sat back.

"Even if..." she said. "You know I can't be responsible for a child. You know what happened." She looked away. "This is impossible."

"You were *not* responsible for that child, Cass. What happened wasn't your fault. And you take wonderful care of the Fates. That's who you are."

Her hands fell to the table.

"We can be a family again," he said. "*I'm* going to take care of the baby. You and me, we can be the same with each other."

Around the bar, people were drinking, talking, walking in and out—behaving as expected.

"We only have one bedroom," she said, as if this were the one thing that could not be overcome.

"Our bedroom is still our bedroom. She's not in there."

"There are so many reasons this will not work," she said. "We should talk about, you know, how to divide—"

"No," he said. "I won't."

His eyes were on her but something was moving, and she looked down to see his hand reaching across the table. All the way across, until it found hers.

And she felt her body give a little in spite of herself. She loved him. She missed him. And she wanted him to force her home against her will because there was no other way for it to happen. Between them stretched a distance she didn't know how to cross.

"It's harder than I thought, taking care of a baby," he said. "I've now knocked on Katie's door as many times as she's knocked on ours. She told me about using the stroller in the house. I can push Amala with my foot while I'm working. But you were right. I didn't understand before. I can't work when I want to. I can't sleep when I want to. My life is going to be different, but yours doesn't have to be. I won't let it."

"Strollers are *not* the life I want."

"I'm done in Afghanistan. I'll be home every night. That's what you wanted, me home at night."

"You have to be home," she said, taking her hand back.

"There *are* good things about a baby. She makes me laugh. Life is slower."

Three businessmen surged into the bar, all in suits.

His body curved toward her. "I want you to have the life you want. I'll make it happen. You can have the life you want even with a baby under the same roof."

"You know that's not true."

"Come by tomorrow and just see. Come for dinner. Just an hour. I'll show you we can do this."

He took her hand again and enclosed it in both of his.

The businessmen roared with laughter. One slapped another on the back.

Again, Cass took her hand back.

"We can make this work," he said. "We always knew it was going to be hard. Each of us knew we weren't going to get everything we wanted."

At that, she stood. "Easy for you to say. You've already gotten what you wanted. In spades." She looked at him, sitting there, this man who had brought strollers into their life, and she hated him. "Now it will *never* be my turn. And all the waiting will *never* have been worth it. And what I'm looking at now is the rest of my life of *not* what I want." The full wine glass still sat on the table, and she knocked it in his direction, the glass breaking, and the wine spilling onto the table and onto him.

"This cannot be undone," she said. "There's no way to fix this. A child is in this world because of what you did."

54

Upstairs, Cass hung the "Do Not Disturb" sign on her door and shut it. At least the baby wasn't hers. At least she had a room of her own—where no mothers or little girls or fathers or babies could get to her, where no choices had to be made.

Her phone rang. Vee. Cass ignored the call. The phone rang again. She turned it off. She closed the drapes. As she crawled into bed, it occurred to her that the one thing worse than having a baby with Ethan had happened—Setara had had the baby with Ethan. She got out of bed and took a Xanax, leaving the bottle by the bed.

But she couldn't sleep. She was afraid that if she closed her eyes, she might wake up to find herself alone in her house, tiptoeing through the room where her mother was asleep on the couch and her father was far away in Afghanistan. Her stomach rumbled and then it stopped rumbling. She watched the clock.

At nine thirty, knocking on the door, knocking so sure of itself that Cass knew it was Vee even without hearing her voice. But Cass didn't move. When Vee started pounding, Cass got up and let her in.

"How did you even know I was in here?"

"You weren't answering my calls. Ethan didn't know where you were. Neither did Singer."

"Jeez."

"Well, that's what you get for going silent on me."

Cass got back in bed, and Vee went around turning on lights. She opened the drapes.

"So what happened?" She sat on the end of the bed, dropped her sandals, and pulled her feet underneath her.

"I shouldn't have trusted him."

"*He* shouldn't have screwed up. The fault is not in the trusting. But I've talked to him, Cass. For a long time. And I've listened to Wheeler talk about him. He loves you. He never loved her. He's a good guy."

"He has a baby with another woman, and he's a good guy?"

"Yes," Vee said. "He's a good guy. And there are good things about a baby."

"That's what he said."

A vacuum cleaner started in the hallway.

"Sorry I haven't asked about you and Wheeler."

Vee shook her head. "I'm the last thing you need to worry about now. Wheeler and I are just getting to know each other, and there's something there that could be more. But the big thing is that I asked Dillon for a divorce."

"Wow." It was too much.

"Being with Wheeler helped me to see beyond Dillon, to see how to stop loving him, how to move on. That things can change."

How to stop loving him.

On Vee's wrist, the tattoo. Permanence inflicted on the body. How often tattoos must be a reminder that nothing was.

"Even if that were the life I wanted," Cass said, "I can't take care of a baby."

"Of course, you can," Vee said. "It's not that hard. And I'll help. I want to help. We can read to her. Teach her to love books. We can figure it out."

"No, Vee," Cass said. "I. Can't. Do. It." On the wall in front of her, a black-and-white photograph of Westside Atlanta before the renovations. Empty buildings and blown-out windows. "You're right. Ethan is the good guy. I'm no better than my mother. I only ever think of myself, and that's who I'll always be."

"There's no bad guy here," Vee said. "I want children. But that doesn't make me unselfish. And not wanting them doesn't make you selfish."

"I did everything I was supposed to," Cass said.

Vee leaned toward her. "Look at me. You are *not* your mother. It won't be the same. You're an entirely different person, a wonderful person. You're you—Cass."

But that wasn't good enough. Atta was wrong. She didn't know the truth. And neither did Vee. Only Ethan. And look what had come of that.

"And Ethan's not your father. He's going to stay home. He's going to take care of the baby. It will be different."

Cass stood. "Be realistic, Vee. He's going to take care of her every minute of every day? I'm going to live in that apartment and have *nothing* to do with his child? It doesn't make sense. And I can *never* take care of a baby. Not for one second." She was back in her childhood kitchen, trapped inside that long-necked pitcher with a swan's neck for a handle. She couldn't breathe.

Vee scooted up and leaned against the headboard. "When I told you that I couldn't protect myself from the man I loved and that I still loved that man, the man who hit me, the shame of it disintegrated. I could breathe."

Cass turned in a circle but there was nowhere to go. She reached inside the sleeves of her shirt, cradling her forearms, and she looked past Vee until she was no longer in her childhood kitchen but bending down, reaching for the rose. "I didn't just see that little girl get hit by the motorcycle, Vee. That day, my mother and I had stopped for gas. From the car, I saw roses in the far corner of the lot. By the intersection. It was a tiny triangle garden with a cherry tree in full bloom and clusters of roses thick with leaves." She looked at Vee. "I loved roses. My grandfather had a rose garden. That was my safe place." The vacuum cleaner stopped. "That day I bent down to smell the roses, and a black dog ran by, and then a little girl in a yellow dress. The wind blew around us and for a second, it was just the three of us. Then a woman screamed. I turned, thinking she was screaming at me. The little girl took off and I thought, *run, you can get away.* And a second later," Cass breathed out, "she was hit by the motorcycle."

"Oh, Cass."

"I could have saved her, Vee. I will always be the little girl, never the one who can save the little girl." And the tears came again. Mounds of them. And Vee stood and put her arms around Cass and held on, and Cass felt as if the accident had just happened and Vee had rushed to the scene so she could stand beside her.

"I would have done the same thing, Cass. Running from an abuser is the right instinct. You were trying to protect her. You were just too young yourself to know there were other dangers. You were trying to keep her safe. Don't you see?"

Tears sprinkled Vee's face. Telling her felt different than telling Ethan, as if he could only *see* it, but Vee could be inside it with her. Cass raised her head, feeling calm.

"Your instinct *was* right." Vee said. "You knew to try to protect her."

And Cass could breathe.

55

For the next week, as if she were recuperating from an illness and needed to build up her strength, Cass took a break from people. Vee understood, and they texted. At Howell, Cass did only what was necessary and then returned to the hotel where she ordered soup, took long baths, put on moisturizer, and watched Netflix in bed. Now her body felt as if things were back in the right places. Her head felt clear, and she could feel her feet on the ground.

When Ella brought in the mail, there was an envelope addressed to Bev. It had been more than three months since the diagnosis. She picked up on the first ring.

"You won't believe it, Cass. I'm in a lounge chair looking at the ocean! In Key West. This was the place we were going first after I retired, and now we're here already. How are you? And how are the Fates? How's Ethan? He should be home for good by now."

Cass should have, but had not, expected this question.

"We're great, Bev. It's so good to hear your voice. Let me know when you come back to Atlanta. We can grab lunch."

Cass hung up feeling strange for not having told Bev the truth but also good. Bev was doing fine. And so was she.

$$\circ \, ^\circ \, \circ$$

When she got up for another coffee, Atta was sitting in the living room on one of the yellow sofas. Cass sat down on the other one.

"What are you doing in here?" Cass asked.

"I was making sure I didn't like this room," Atta said.

"And?"

"I really don't. It's stuffy. There's a lot of light, but these couches won't let you relax. And the Betsy Ross painting is too old and dark."

"*Is* there such a thing as too old?"

Atta laughed, not a bit of red lipstick on her white teeth, her long braid hanging to her chest. "That's a new shirt, isn't it?" Atta said. "Kind of hippy-ish. I like it."

"I do, too." Cass had bought it over the weekend. White, billowy long sleeves with all colors of tiny flowers embroidered across the front.

"I was about your age in the sixties. Old Bob was right. The times did change. That was my favorite decade, I think."

"Tell me why."

"Kids were standing up for what they believed in. Not just doing what the grown-ups said. I was in between. Freed me to do what I wanted."

"I thought you'd always done what you wanted."

Atta laughed again. "Leaning toward it, that's for sure."

"Have you already walked?"

"Lois and I went from here. Up and down the street over and over again. I prefer going from one place to another place, but that's not terribly convenient anymore."

"Well, let's think. You could walk from here to somewhere, and Ella or I could come get you."

Atta looked at Cass as if she were going to take no foolishness. "How are you doing at solving your own problems?"

"I am enough," Cass said.

"Good. How's Ethan?"

"I don't know. I'm enough so I don't need him. I booked my room at the hotel for a month."

Atta sat up to the edge of the sofa. "But I told you. You are enough, and you don't have to prove it. *I am enough* is step one. Step two, go forth into the world." Atta raised her hands out to the side.

"You didn't say that."

"I gave you a little credit, but I can spell it out. Sweet Jesus. Now that you know you're enough, you don't need that from Ethan. You can listen to him. You can really listen to another person when you don't need something yourself. So, step two, talk to Ethan."

There was a knock at the front door, and Cass got up to answer it.

"Jana, come in."

"You're looking well, Cass."

Which made Cass cringe. She'd had a shower was all. And the new shirt.

"I'm sorry to come so close to lunchtime," she said, standing in the foyer, "but I was driving by and had the urge to stop."

"I'm glad you did. Atta and I are in the living room. Around here, we don't eat until 12:30 or 1:00. Actually, we don't eat until Fanny says the food is ready."

Jana smiled and preceded Cass into the living room.

Atta scooted over. "Sit by me," she said.

"I'd love to," Jana said. "It's so lovely and light in here."

"I was just saying that to Cass, the light part. Otherwise, I think it's a bit too stuffy."

"How's everything going?" Jana asked, looking from Cass to Atta.

Afraid Atta was going to detail her personal history, Cass jumped in. "Atta and Lois have been out to exercise today. May is still in bed but no worse. Fanny is trying a new recipe tonight—one of Ella's mother's Spanish dishes, so we have that to look forward to. And we've raised another $12,000."

Which, after Cass said it, didn't seem like so much in the scheme of things, but it was moving in the right direction.

"How's your son doing?" Atta asked.

"I'm on the way to meet him for lunch. He's quiet, but he talks to me while he eats." She smiled. "And I've been talking to my friends about this place. Told them you needed money. None of them had heard of it. I think there may be some untapped sources out there."

"Oh, my gosh, thank you so much, Jana. That's awesome."

Jana looked at her watch. "I should go. May I take a few brochures with me?"

"Absolutely," Cass said. "I'll get them." While she was putting them in a large envelope, Cass heard Fanny call that lunch was ready.

When Cass appeared in the foyer, Atta headed down the hall, waving at Jana.

"See you next time, Atta." Jana opened the front door then turned back to Cass. "I'm not sure who Ethan is, but Atta said you *have to* talk to him."

56

Time and Atta were softening her edges. The next time Ethan called, Cass stared at the phone, at his name and that face she missed, and she thought about answering. The next day when he called, she did.

"How about a walk?" he said. "Tomorrow morning? It's Saturday. I could meet you outside your hotel, and we could get a latte."

Looking out the hotel window at the little bit of sky she could see, she said, "Why don't you bring the baby?" But then she had a vision of him wearing her in one of those backpack things and added, "In the stroller."

$$\circ \, ^{\circ} \circ$$

At ten the next day, they had to move the coffee to two because Amala was napping and then she'd need lunch. Cass waited until five past to make sure she wasn't standing on the sidewalk waiting for him. That would make her think too much.

"Hey," he said, the stroller on the other side of him so the baby was facing away from her.

Cass tried to smile but swallowed instead. "I should probably say hello to her."

Ethan wheeled her around, and the minute Amala saw her, she smiled.

"I told her to do that," he said.

Cass laughed and thought okay, maybe the walk would be fine. After they got their lattes, they headed toward the library. Amala fell asleep, and she and Ethan made mostly small talk—he asked about Howell and the fund-raising, she asked about his work.

"I thought I would miss it," he said. "I thought I would miss the people, the air, the ground. I didn't think I could be me without Afghanistan."

Cass looked at him.

"But I don't miss Afghanistan. The only thing I miss is you."

He stopped and she stopped, and there was nothing between them.

"It's so empty in the apartment without you," he said. "I'm sorry. I didn't know—I didn't understand—what it felt like."

Her shell cracked a bit. She hadn't realized the situation had reversed itself.

When he touched her arm, she didn't pull away, and when he touched her cheek, she let him. His fingers felt just as she remembered.

One step at a time. Maybe she could do this. If Ethan really was going to take care of the baby. If she really weren't responsible.

They continued on and turned around just short of the library when it started to sprinkle. But when they turned, the stroller hit a bump in the sidewalk and jarred the baby awake, and she cried. And that jarred something in Cass. Of course, she would be responsible, too—she would be the baby's mother. Her mother.

And something that had felt right side up turned upside down again. This was the moment *her* mother had prepared her for, the moment she was supposed to be strong. And Cass *was* going to be strong but not the way her mother had meant. She would not do to Amala what had been done to her. She would not start this long journey just because a little girl needed taking care of. Something had to be different. She would not allow herself to be a part of this little girl's life without wanting her.

57

Cass shuffled through the dwindling rain, searching but finding no answers in the faces of the people she passed. Despite the weather, the sidewalks were full. She walked for a while, knowing that would calm her, and then she veered toward the bar. Vee only wanted to find a bright side and there was no bright side here. Singer usually opened, but she didn't know when. If he wasn't there, she would wait.

The bar was dark, the bar stools empty, not a bit of life anywhere. As if it might never open again. Across from the bar, the covered patio was deserted. But there were crumbs surrounded by ants, a balled-up wrapper beside the trash can, an eight-ounce glass Coke bottle abandoned on a picnic table at the other end of the patio dwarfed by its surroundings, as if as tall as it could be was just not good enough.

Cass wanted to pick up the trash, but instead she just sat in the middle of all these things that had been left behind. After a minute, she lifted her legs over the bench and deposited them under the table. She slid her purse underneath her head as it fell to the tabletop. She closed her eyes and a minute later felt the relief of coming sleep.

$$\circ \, ^{\circ} \, \circ$$

When she opened her eyes, Singer was sitting beside her and yet nowhere near her, straddling the bench as if it were a horse, his hands on his legs.

"Vee told me," he said. "I'm sorry."

She raised her head and pain shot through her neck. "I don't want to be strong," she said, rubbing her neck.

"I'm sure Ethan doesn't care if you're strong or not."

"I have to be strong," she said to this man, his eyes dark with sunglasses.

"Throw the have-to's out," he said, clasping his hands in front of him. "What do you want?"

"For you to take off your glasses."

He removed them, flicking his hair to the side as she remembered boys in high school doing. He placed the glasses on the table. He wore his hair longer now than when she'd first met him.

"You have green eyes," she said. "With specks of gold in them."

"My mother calls them hazel."

"I hardly know anything about you, and yet here is where I came." She straddled the bench, facing him.

"Maybe that's why you came," he said.

"Singer," a waitress shouted from the other side of the patio.

He held up one finger without looking away. "What's your heart saying to you?"

"I don't know," she said. "There's too much."

"According to my mother, no matter how much there is, the question is always love or freedom."

To stay or to go.

He brought his leg from underneath the table. Then he stood and offered his hand, which she took. And she stood and looked deep into his hazel eyes, searching for what, she wasn't sure. "Do I matter to you?" she asked.

"You know you do," he said, squeezing her hand. "But you also know you matter to Ethan. And I'm afraid at this moment, you're here because I'm not Ethan. Because we have no history, no past. Because it's easy. And that's okay by me. But it's not the same as coming here for me. As wanting me."

Instinctively, she looked toward the pedestrian bridge. Higher ground was what she needed. Perspective.

"But if it's me you want," Singer said, pulling her to him and holding her close—and she wanted someone to hold her close. He kissed her forehead, quick and light. "I *am* easy," he said.

Which made her feel as if everything would be okay, and as if nothing would be okay ever again.

Singer put his arm around her and led her toward the bar, but she checked behind her as if she might have forgotten something.

$$\circ \, ^{\circ} \, \circ$$

Cass didn't sit at her normal spot but all the way around on the far side of the counter where the waitresses came to collect their drink orders. And where she could see the door. She dreaded Vee's arrival, but Vee did not arrive. A little before six, Cass and Singer each got a text. *Don't worry about me. With Wheeler looking at airstream trailers. :)*

She was happy for Vee. But something else was mixed in, too—strands of sadness and longing. For what the beginning was and what now was not. Relationships changed over the years. She knew that.

"I can't do it out of a sense of duty," she said.

"People say you're at the mercy of your feelings," Singer said, pulling coasters from a package and stacking them, "but I'm not so sure about that. I think you can harness them, like the wind."

"I have to want it."

"That may be right," he said, "for you. For someone else, duty might be just the ticket. Vee uses fear."

"Were you scared when you heard the fighting at Vee's, when Dillon hit her?"

Singer took his pen from his pocket and pulled a coaster from one of the stacks. He drew her. No smile. But her eyes looked less wide and deeper now. Her cheeks fit her face better. Perhaps she was growing into herself.

Like a magic trick, he slipped the drawing of her underneath her glass and removed the blank coaster. "I was scared," he said, "but that didn't matter. I heard a crash and Vee's scream. I could hear him yelling at her. My mother was already reaching for her key. I took it, having no idea what I'd find. I do remember thinking he might have a gun. You know, you hope you'll do the right thing, but you never know until you're in it. I don't like conflict. I never have. I never will. But it's where you discover what matters. What's important to you. If you emerge, you emerge better or worse. Never the same. And you learn things about yourself. Sometimes you're ready for what you learn; sometimes not."

Cass reached for Singer, her fingers lighting on his forearm but not sticking, and as she leaned forward, her feet touched the ground. Goosebumps from her shoulders to her hands, from her chest to her feet. In that moment, she saw him. Her friend. And she saw how he was a bright and shiny thing, a sharp object, her way out but not the reason to come out.

She wrapped both hands around her still half-full glass.

He popped the counter with his hand and then slid to the other end of the bar to take an order.

It wasn't dark yet but outside, lights were coming on. Inside, servers were lighting the candles on the tables. The music got louder. Bon Iver. "Beth/Rest," the stripped-down Rare Book Room version. That voice, the sound of sadness. *Pry it open with your love.* But the piano key in the background, constant. That one key. Over and over again. The sadness that was almost too much. But that key, insistent. Then the lightness, the hope.

58

Two days after her walk with Ethan, Cass noticed the pass to the exercise studio on the corner of the desk and, thinking maybe she had walked enough, grabbed it up. Core had tall, warehouse ceilings, exposed pipes, brick walls, and huge glass windows that showed the orange and pink slivers of the sun about to set. It was empty of people and smelled of eucalyptus. She asked for Finn and told him that her body ached as it had when she was a child. Growing pains, her father had always said.

"I need to stretch. That's what it feels like I need."

But Finn, a master trainer, suggested Gyrotonics. "It's stretching," he said, "with lots of twisting and turning that will make you feel just groovy." As he came around the counter, he said, "And bonus, it's also strength training."

Finn was tall and lean with sharp features that reminded her of Mick Jagger. He told her that Gyrotonics was a method of exercise developed by a professional dancer from Romania, to heal himself after injuries. He asked if she were a reader, and she nodded.

"I knew it. I can always tell."

As he turned levers and adjusted a tall machine connected to a black bench, he said, "Truman Capote. I'm reading everything in order. And I'm up to *Breakfast at Tiffany's*. But I just can't get past that first line. "I am always drawn back to places where I have lived, the houses and their neighborhoods."

"I've never read it," she said. "Just seen the movie, which I love."

"Sit," he said.

She straddled a bench and faced him.

"Reach your arms out."

When she did, he adjusted a little more. "I'm going home on Friday," he said. "New Orleans like Capote. I think it's the only thing. Then, I hope, forward." He stood. "Okay, rest your palms on top of the handles and push out to your full wingspan."

"I can barely reach the handles," she said.

"You're just moving your arms. Try moving from your core."

And the next thing she knew he was sitting behind her, his hands on her hips, rolling her forward, then back. "Feel it here first," he said, his fingers pressing out from her hips into her stomach. "With Gyrotonics, you're learning to move from a new place. Now look how far you can reach."

And she could reach farther. It surprised her. Still, she kept having to stop and start over. *Stop thinking*, she told herself, and closed her eyes, and when she let her body go, it knew what to do. She felt tendons and muscles and bones she was sure she'd never felt before.

"You're moving in multiple dimensions," Finn said. "Do you feel it? Up and down, left and right, backward and forward, space and time. The fundamental link. Einstein and all that."

59

In the hospital, Cass sat beside May's bed, holding *The Heart Is a Lonely Hunter* open to where they'd left off just a few days before. The nurse had told her she doubted May would make it through the night. May, who had never seemed lonely, but who, if it weren't for Cass, would be dying all alone, which, Ella had reminded Cass when she'd called, would not have bothered May.

But it should have bothered her. May was always Harvey, Harvey, Harvey. "Don't get me wrong," May had said. "I'm not ready. But I love that it's my heart sending me on my way. Harvey would have appreciated that, too." They would ship May's body to Dayton, Ohio, to be buried next to Harvey. May had said it wasn't worth the effort, or the money. But she had promised him.

Well, where was Harvey now?

May's breathing was raspy. She was taking in less air, letting even less out.

Strength. Cass held onto the world by strength. And if her feelings tried to suggest otherwise, she buried them. Sealed them off and moved on. Without her strength, she had nothing. Without her strength, she was her mother.

And yet, what Cass felt now was not strength but sadness—that knot in her chest. She felt it loosening and unraveling into so many threads she couldn't follow them all.

She was used to life being snatched away. She was used to death arriving suddenly and without warning. How oddly disorienting to know it was coming. To sit with it. To witness the slow ticks away from life. To know that life had not been interrupted but had come to its natural conclusion.

Cass had planned to read to May here in the hospital even if she couldn't understand. But she hadn't yet read a word. When she glanced down, she saw that the corners of the book had seared indentations into her palms. These would be May's last pages. Maybe Cass should skip to the end.

She stood. Cass had listened to May and felt her own heart. And when she had read to May, she had heard her own voice. She'd never been able to figure out what May needed because May hadn't needed anything. It was Cass who had needed May.

Her face looked as soft and thin as a baby's blanket. Cass bent down close. How could there be that many wrinkles in so small an area. And a tiny scar on May's jawline next to her ear that Cass had never noticed before. She reached out and smoothed her finger over it. May's breath across her wrist. Cass slid her fingers across May's cheeks, her chin, her forehead. And May's face seemed to drop a little, to relax. Cass opened her hand and feathered four fingers in a circular motion around May's face and up and down her neck. May seemed more peaceful. And Cass leaned down and kissed the downy top of her head. And that's when Cass understood. May wasn't alone even before Cass had arrived. Harvey was always with her. Still gently taking that bird off her head.

She sat down and turned to where they'd left off. "Page 174," she said aloud.

60

The next morning the phone rang. Ella. Cass dressed quickly, wanting to get to Howell. May had died, and she wanted to be with them.

Once there, she went straight to the hall closet and pulled the toolbox off the top shelf. Ella and Fanny came out of the kitchen, Atta and Lois behind them. In the living room, Cass stopped in front of the window where she and May had first sat. She found the putty knife and ran it along the edge between the window and the frame, and at each corner of the window, she stuck it in and with a hammer, wedged it in further. She'd watched her father do this a thousand times. She straightened and dropped the tools in the box. When she wiggled the window, it moved. She placed a hand on each side and pushed up. As the window gave, there was a swoosh, and Cass let it pull her against the screen. Then she felt the fresh air pour into her, and she felt her lungs expanding.

○ ○ ○

Later, in her office with the door shut, after talking to the director at the funeral home, Cass opened the bottom drawer, dug for the manila file folder, and dropped it on top of her desk. This part of the job fell into the same category as raising money—things she didn't like to do. But these things came with the pleasure of being in charge.

Still, the air was too thick with the sadness of May's death for Cass to be able to look forward to a new Fate. For as long as she'd been at Howell, May had been here. She stood, not knowing what would come next.

Since Cass had been in charge, she'd known May was dying. Known she would eventually have to open this folder. Bev always said she notified the next person on the waiting list as soon as possible—as much for her own sake as anything else.

Since she'd been in charge.

Cass eyed the folder. Then she scooped it up and put it back in the drawer. As she was heading to be with the others, she heard a knock at the front door.

Jana. "Atta called. I'm so sorry, Cass."

"Come on in," Cass said.

"I just wanted to be here. I know I haven't known you all long, that I'm not a part of—"

"Sure you are. I'm glad you came. Let's join everyone in the kitchen."

○ ○ ○

It was the end of the day before Cass ever went back to her office. When she sat down at her desk, a fat envelope sat on top of her papers, her name on it, printed in blue ink she was relieved to see.

As Cass picked it up, she noticed Atta standing by the door and waved her in, suspecting Atta might know something about the envelope.

Inside, a note and a stack of checks.

Cass,

I only spoke to May once, but I know there will be such sadness today at Howell. Here's what I have so far—I wanted you all to see a way forward.

Love, Jana

The first check, $20,000. Cass placed it facedown on her desk. Then $20,000 again, and over and over. Until the last one, the thirteenth check. As she took it in, she felt the same soft thing she'd felt reading the notice on the library bulletin board so many years ago. That soft feeling was a sense of peace, she realized, the same thing she'd felt talking to May. As if she'd found something that had been missing and she could rest now. Her shoulders dropped, and she breathed out.

"Well?" Atta asked.

Cass picked up the stack and handed it over.

Atta began to count, putting each check in her lap. And when she got to the last one, she looked up grinning. "A $100,000 from Jana!" Atta put her hand on her chest. "Why, Lord Jesus, we almost have it all. And it's only June!"

Cass felt a shift—from contentment to something else. The corners of her mouth turned skyward, and she felt her eyes sparkling. "We're going to do it, Atta. We're going to save Howell."

"I need to move around," Atta said, scooping up the checks and handing them back to Cass. "That's a lot of excitement. I won't say a word. I'll let you tell the others."

"Thanks, Atta, for all you did to make this happen."

"I didn't do anything," Atta said, at the door. Then she turned and stuck her head back in. "By the way, I thought you knew. If May told me once, she told me a thousand times. It was you." Atta stood there for a second longer. "You made the difference here, Cass."

Out the windows, a gust of wind set the branches and leaves in motion. From where Cass sat, it looked like a celebration. Howell House was going to make it. She had the urge to stand up and twirl. *Joy*, she thought. *This must be joy.*

○ ○ ○

On her way back to the hotel, her sadness returned, but even with the addition of May's death, it didn't seem as big as before. It wasn't taking up all the room in her body. They were working together to save Howell, and that was inside her, too.

In front of her, an old milk carton rolled across the pavement. Before she got to the trash can, she'd also picked up a piece of some sort of map and a pink hair band. As she tossed the things in, there on the ground was a single green flip-flop. It wasn't red like the one that had washed up on the breakwater that day in Provincetown, but it was the match nonetheless.

She looked up, and then turned right instead of left.

61

Cass had never really studied their door—this rectangular block of wood that had stopped her so completely. If only it were made of some softer substance that would have slowed her progress rather than halting it. On the street, it had all seemed so easy. As if she really had crossed some bridge and could now walk over here and talk to Ethan without anger, without fear. But the euphoria of knowing that was what she wanted and needed to do had evaporated and been replaced by this piece of painted blue wood.

Using her key didn't feel right. But the longer she stood here, the less confidence she had, and before she lost another drop, she raised her arm and knocked.

When the door opened, there was cold air. And Ethan, smiling at her.

"Where's the baby?" she asked.

"Sleeping."

"Where?"

"The guest bathroom."

She laughed, surprising herself, and then she looked from the man in front of her, back to the strong wooden door frame, and finally to the newly created opening. And she stepped into the apartment.

"I thought I'd just pick up a few things, visit for a minute."

"Next time you come," he said, "maybe you could bring some things back."

She waited a second, but it felt good to hear him say that. Nothing but good.

Around the room, blurry gray light poured in. A pink blanket lay folded over the arm of the TV sofa, and a green-and-white slinky-type toy was hooked to the bottom of the coffee table. More things, fewer edges.

The baby began to cry, and Ethan went to get her. Cass followed, but stopped where the den and dining room narrowed into the hallway. On the dining room table, Ethan had lit one of her scented candles, and the room smelled of bergamot and mint. Then Ethan was standing in front of her, in their apartment, holding a baby girl wrapped in a yellow blanket.

The baby smiled at her.

"Look at that," Ethan said. "She did it again. And she doesn't smile often."

Don't try to make it disappear, she told herself.

"Hey there," she said to Amala.

Cass looked into their faces. Nobody ran anywhere. Everyone was safe.

Ethan came closer, with the baby. He touched her arm and took the baby into the den. She stayed where she was. There was her green jacket with the tie in the back hanging on the coat rack. At the other end of the hall, there was her desk. At the threshold to their bedroom, she stopped and leaned on the thick ridges of the door molding. The alarm clock. The wall of windows. She had no idea how long she'd been standing there when she heard something and turned to see Ethan inching the bathroom door closed.

He seemed comfortable, settled in. His eyes stayed on her instead of jumping to something else. It was the early Ethan, his arms loose by his sides and an open space in front of him. And like a line of cold air in a house where all the windows and doors were closed, Cass felt something. Something that lifted her up and threw her down at the same time. The baby cried. But Ethan's arms were around her, and she smelled that verbena soap she'd bought for the shower in another lifetime.

"I'm not going anywhere," he said, his cheek on her head. He smoothed her hair.

The baby stopped crying.

He held her close and kissed her hair and her cheek, and she turned toward him, and he kissed her—so lightly she touched her lips as if searching for proof.

"I don't know if I can..." she said.

He shook his head and took her hands. "*I* can, babe. Let me. Let me be here. And let me take care of you for a while."

Something released in her chest, creating a little spot where she could stand to feel the movement.

"As long as you're with me," he said, "I can do anything. I'll figure out about Amala. It will be all me."

$$\circ \, ^{\circ} \, \circ$$

As he walked her to the door, he said, "Being at home with Amala, I've been thinking about your dad."

"My dad? Why?"

"I want to protect her from everything."

"Things were great when my dad was home."

"But he left you with your mother."

"He didn't know how bad it was. When he was home, my mother was in heaven. They idolized each other. We were all happy. Which made me feel like this dark thing that happened when he wasn't around. I...I made her unhappy. He made her happy."

"I just feel like he should have known somehow. That he has a part to play in how bad it was when he wasn't there."

She considered this, thinking back. "I wanted to be like him. Chin up and all that. To complain would have been to be like her. I never told him."

He held her again. "I'm sorry, Cass." And he kept his hand on her back as she slipped her messenger bag across her body. "I'm sorry I wasn't here for you more."

She touched his arm, then reached to open the door.

"Oh, I have something for you," he said. "I can't believe I almost forgot." And he reached in his pocket and handed her something.

"A rock?"

"Granite," he said.

62

Darkness, like an incoming tide, made a tinier and tinier island of the well-lit café patio where Cass sat across from her old apartment, but she no longer felt as if she were clinging to the light. She no longer felt stranded; she felt comfortable. And although the darkness weakened her ability to see into the distance, it strengthened her ability to see the lights that were out there. One had already been turned on in her old window by the maple tree.

When she'd moved in after her father's death, she'd felt relieved to get out of the dorm and to be able to shut a door behind her. Now she felt safe out here, and yet a thread of emptiness was still with her, but the feeling wasn't desperate as it had been then, just familiar.

Cass looked around—she was the only one left on the patio. And she didn't care. She had come here because after being with Ethan and Amala, she couldn't stand the thought of another meal in her room watching TV or in the hotel restaurant with those green walls. She liked being outside, even if it was warm. She held tight to the granite, its rough edges reminding her of so much. Out here, her feelings had the space they needed.

The waiter, dressed in French fashion in black pants, white shirt, white apron, leaned against the rolling cart next to the door. He glanced her way periodically, acting as if he didn't see her and reminding her of a waiter she'd had in Paris. She'd gone to the same café every morning for a week—her father eating in his room at dawn—but that waiter never acknowledged he'd ever seen her before.

A shadow crossed the window of the apartment where she had believed Ethan would always be faithful and always keep his word. Now she sat out here in the world where people cheated and broke agreements. But Vee was right—the past would never be any different. And the future would never be happily ever after. Cass had known that as a fact, and now she knew it in her heart. She lived in the same world as everyone else.

She breathed out those words—the same world as everyone else.

The disconnection and loneliness she'd been lugging around all her life could have been the end of her, but she'd kept going, looking without seeing, doing the next thing. All those years ago, the leaves on the tree had been budding and celery green. Whoever was in the apartment brushed by the window again, came back, and stood in front of it. Cass couldn't tell whether it was a man or a woman, the tree now full of dark green leaves, mature leaves. Its most glorious season still to come.

She didn't understand why she'd so desperately wanted Ethan to be her whole world, why she'd wanted him all to herself. And then she saw her mother, sitting in the kitchen, smoking a cigarette and waiting. But she had run past her mother and out the door. Yet she had become her mother all the same.

That one-bedroom apartment on the other side of the tree was the last place she had lived alone. The only place she had lived alone. Which was difficult to believe. Hadn't she always been alone?

Until Ethan.

Sitting here by herself, she felt relief, as if she lived in a large full house, a large full world, and had snuck away by herself for a few moments of reprieve. She was dreading going back to her small hotel room. Maybe she would stay a little longer, have another glass of wine, and she motioned to the waiter, who was in his sixties maybe, bald and pudgy.

"All by yourself tonight?" he asked, as he approached.

"I didn't think waiters were supposed to say things like that."

"You're correct," he said. "Tonight, you are a party of one?"

She smiled. "Could I get another glass of wine?"

He smiled, too, dipping his head in acknowledgment. "Forgive me," he said, as he headed inside. Then he turned back. "And might I add that you are quite a beautiful party of one."

63

Back in her hotel room, the sheets were cold as she settled in bed with her computer. Opening photos, she pulled up the one that she supposed still lay facedown on her desk, the one Wheeler had taken at their wedding—Ethan reaching for her and she just out of his reach. And she thought of the minister with the tie-dyed T-shirt underneath his robe.

Three words, he had said. *My gift to you—perfect love forgiveness.* He'd said them just like that there in front of the altar. In less than a minute, the minister gave his blessing. It was impossible to be perfect and love was bigger than any one action and something about wading through a river with forgiveness being the way to the other side.

She could be angry and sad and unhappy—she could be her mother—or she could forgive him.

Looking up, she saw nothing but that blur when a thought is too much.

She blinked. Where was Rumi? She closed her computer and took the book off the bedside table. When she dropped it on the bed, it fell open, as it always did, to one of her father's underlined passages.

Your body is a stingy piece of aloeswood
that won't let go its healing smoke
until you put it in the fire.

Aloeswood (as a little girl she'd thought her father was saying *hallowed woods*) was a heartwood. It formed in response to infection. The sicker the tree got, the darker and more aromatic the center became.

She turned out the lamp and sat there. In the darkness, she let her arms fall to the side. If she could just let go of the controls. And as she felt the blood flow to her hands, the walls fell away. Her body expanded and came alive—the backs of her legs, under her forearms whatever that was called, her cheeks down close to her jawbone. When she leaned her head against the headboard and stretched, she felt a rush and heard her father's words and voice. *You will always have a choice.*

She sat up, placing her feet on the floor, as alert as if she'd heard someone trying to get in the room.

Over in the closet was her old rolling tapestry suitcase, empty and ready to be filled, ready to take her far from here.

Or back home.

She did, in fact, have a choice.

She could walk away—choosing the life she wanted over the man she loved—or she could stay—choosing the man she loved over the life she wanted. She couldn't have it all. She couldn't even have what she was owed. But she had a choice. And she knew what she wanted more than anything else.

Gamble everything for love.

But if she went back, there would be three of them. *Three.* At the end of the day, he had still slept with another woman and now had a child. He had ruined their plans. She didn't know how to forgive him.

She went to the window and pulled back the drapes—darkness spilled everywhere. No moon, no stars, only tiny sparkles of light from inside other buildings and from the street. She raised the window, but it only opened six inches. She needed to breathe out—all the way. Her body had been running inefficiently, getting plenty of oxygen but not getting rid of enough carbon dioxide. She pushed to empty her lungs. Bending down, she turned her head sideways and exhaled over and over again. She heard the whistle of the wind, the call of a siren, a dog barking. She closed her eyes for a minute, and the voices swirled around inside her—her mother's, her father's, her grandfather's, Ethan's, the voices in books, in songs, in instruments, and in the world. She heard it all and imagined reaching for just one thing, and when she opened her hand, what she saw was the want—the want she herself had created wanting her mother to want her. A word that could go either way.

She straightened, blood returning to the places it belonged, and she felt herself emerging from something she'd been wrapped in for years and years. Something that had kept her safe while her wounds healed and she grew up. As much as she wanted her mother to want her, that was never going to happen, and she was ready to let it go. She would take all that need, all that want, and turn it around, toward this baby Ethan loved—wanting her to grow up strong and wanting her to survive. And this time, *she* was the grown-up. She could save the little girl.

The water rose up over the breakwater, poured over the passage, flooding her heart, scattering debris, erasing the marks of the past, but the giant boulders held. It wouldn't be easy, but something new was opening before her, showing her all that was possible, showing her how the water, despite the stones, could flow through, around, and forward.

The wind rattled the window. Her heart pitched. It wasn't just about the little girl. But she wouldn't be able to forgive Ethan until she could forgive herself.

Her mistake had taken a little girl out of this life.

Eyeing the hotel window's narrow opening, she thought of that tattoo on Vee's wrist, the tiny bird flying up and down, and up again, and she remembered the black-headed, orange-beaked tern from all those years ago on the tidal flats. She slid her wrist through the opening in the window, and she opened her hand and let the bird go, let it float up and down with the wind, no resistance, no fear, only the wild pleasure of possibility. Maybe if she could forgive Ethan, she could learn to forgive herself. The wind dropped, revealing something else, and her hand dropped with it but stayed out there on the ledge. She *could* forgive Ethan. He might be the only person in the whole world she could forgive. Why had it taken so long for her to see?

His mistake had brought a little girl into this life.

Her hand lifted, and the wind ran through her fingers and around her wrist. She felt her heart pulsing inside her chest. She would not be her mother. She could forgive Ethan, and then she could forgive herself. And if she could forgive herself, maybe she could learn to forgive her mother. After all, her father had loved her mother. Cass would look for the good things.

Forgiveness. Like that ride where you swirl so fast, you stick to the side, the bottom falls out, and you're free.

64

Cass sat on the sofa, and Ethan brought the baby, who was chubby and watchful and seemed to seldom cry. He placed her in front of them in some sort of baby seat—an imperfect triangle.

"Does her name mean something?"

"Her real name is Amal—which means 'hope' in Arabic. But early on, Setara took to calling her Amala—which means 'bird' or 'beloved.'"

"That's lovely," Cass said.

Ethan looked at his watch and reached to pick her up. "I didn't realize it was time to fix her bottle."

"You can leave her," Cass said, watching her, having no idea what might happen next.

Above the fireplace, the two photos of the girls. *The one in gray, determined to survive; the one in the rose-colored scarf, stronger than she yet knew.* Ethan was here, and she had noticed the paintings.

Leaning forward with intention, she rubbed her finger up and down the baby's soft, fat leg. She could wrap her whole hand around it, which she did, and she held on. Then she felt a tug and saw that the baby had grabbed her finger. And something about that tug reminded Cass of a little girl she had known long ago, a little girl who lay in a dark closet wanting to wake up in the forest with the talking elephants who tore the darkness to shreds. And her own little girl tears wiggled out from underneath her dresses where she had stuffed them. This wasn't what she'd wanted. And she knew it wasn't what Ethan had wanted either. But maybe it was exactly what she needed.

Cass breathed out. Perhaps she'd gotten to the end of the

tears now, and as she had the thought, she understood that there would be no end to tears and that there would be tears of all sorts. The Fates had tried to tell her. The unexpected was something to hope for. Spilling was what she needed to do, what she would surely do again.

She reached for the little girl.

With her hands underneath the baby, she lifted her, aware of the additional weight, but equally strong was the weight inside her. She started down the hallway. At the threshold to their room, she paused. Their bed. Her desk. Wedding photo right side up.

Cass held Amala close, her hand on the back of her head, and stepped across, into their room where she sat and propped the baby against her chest, facing the desk. Cass reached out and rested her hand on the wood; she breathed out, relaxing into the space around her. She could do this.

In her lap, a tuft of black curls sticking straight up. Amala began to fuss, and Cass knew to sing. *Silent Night*. She lifted a brass handle and let it fall and bent down to look at her. The baby smiled, her eyes full of light. Cass raised and dropped the brass handle again, and the baby smiled again. One more time. Three times, like always.

Ethan came up beside her with the bottle in his hand. He placed his hand on her shoulder and kissed the top of her head. Then he picked up Amala. Cass listened to them leave the room. Ethan loved her and she loved him, and this little girl with the obsidian curls and no mother was his little girl.

She knew what it felt like to be that little girl.

"Ethan," she called.

He came back into the room, still holding Amala.

"What if I wanted to help you with her?"

He tilted his head in her direction, a smile starting at the corners of his mouth.

Cass smiled, too.

There were so many things about this man she had yet to discover. And a whole new person she knew nothing about in his arms. But she knew one thing.

"You know we'll have to take her back sometime, so she can see it for herself."

65

In the huge expanse of the park, with the leaves on the trees more golden, more rust, more burgundy each day, at a distance but within her sight, a man and a baby—her husband and their child. Ethan pushed Amala, who was leaning forward in the stroller, toward the pond. The ducks were already squawking. He stopped and looked behind him, and Cass watched him find her just off the path, watched him raise his camera and shoot. He smiled and continued on. At the edge of the pond, he pulled out the stale bread, tore off a piece, and threw it into the water, drawing the ducks to them. He gave Amala a piece to throw in, but she put it in her mouth, as Cass knew she would.

Despite the large grassy area between them, Cass felt as if she stood on the edge of something she didn't understand to which she was holding too tightly. Parts of her still felt as if she were bracing herself. She dropped her jaw and softened her eyes. Maybe fear was why she still, months out, had been unable to navigate the distance that remained. Fear of what, she couldn't imagine. Of letting go her hold on the universe, of what might happen if she did.

Above her, the low, unending fall blue sky. Two birds swooped over and all the way to the pond, where they skirted the water, showing off. She followed the birds but picked up Amala pointing and looking up, her head falling to the back of the stroller and resting there, watching the birds as they played. The little girl twisted in her stroller. The birds were headed back toward Cass, who turned as they flew over her again and disappeared into the trees behind her. When she turned back around, Amala, black curls framing her face, was watching her, waiting it seemed.

What must she be thinking?

Cass took a step toward her and was about to take another when a gust of wind kicked up, unlocking something inside her. She opened her fists. Her next step felt springy, and the next gust brought with it a line of cool air. The squawking ducks got louder, thunderous like elephants. She threw her head back, smiling. The cool forest where the talking elephants lived—she had finally found it. And she held her arms out to the side, closed her eyes, and let the wind lift her. The squawking became music, the trumpet sound of all those elephants waiting all this time. And she twirled and twirled and twirled, one breeze leading to the next that led to the next, like waves rushing in, overlapping, until Cass felt as if she were a part of it all.

Acknowledgments

On a cold day in January of 2013, as I headed to Provincetown to begin a new novel—the idea floating in my head that one of the characters would have some connection to Afghanistan—I found myself sitting next to Michael Sheridan, the Director of Community Supported Film, an organization that trains local storytellers in conflicted and developing countries. He was on his way home after spending three months in Afghanistan and graciously spent the entire flight sharing his photos and talking to me about the country and its people. It was a mystical moment, and I owe him for setting the book on its way.

Steve McCurry's famous photograph *Afghan Girl* also inspired me, and I'm appreciative of the complexity and boldness of his images that lend themselves to a myriad of imaginings.

In addition, two texts were inspirational as I was writing this book—*The Essential Rumi*, edited by Coleman Barks, and *The Heart Is a Lonely Hunter* by Carson McCullers.

Many thanks to the Ragdale Foundation, Vermont College of Fine Arts, Writing by Writers, and Catching Days and its readers, all of whom have provided a place for my writing, bolstered my confidence as a writer, and made me feel part of a community.

I'm grateful to the following people for reading drafts of the novel and encouraging both my writing and my spirits: Katie Shea Boutillier, Dani Shapiro, Jodi Paloni, Sarah Stone, and Jay Schaefer.

Thank you to the good people at Mango Publishing for this paperback edition, with special thanks to Morgane Leoni who redesigned the interior and the cover.

I am particularly indebted to my editor, Lisa McGuinness, whose suggestions exerted just the right pressure at just the right angle to enable me to speed up or slow down, to dig deeper or wider and who just might be my perfect editor. Thank you for loving the manuscript, seeing all it could be, and turning it into a real book. Thanks also to Amy Bauman for her sharp copyediting skills, to Rose Wright for her lovely design work, to Donna Linden for proofreading with a vengeance, and extra special thanks to my son Jack Martin for creating the hardback cover I adore.

I'd like to thank my brilliant friend, Pam Houston, whose writing and wisdom have set the bar high high high and who has shaped me as a writer and as a human being.

Thank you to my family and friends who have supported and encouraged me throughout my writing years. In particular, thanks to Amandah Turner, my best *reader reader*, and to Karen Nelson, my best *writer reader*. Thank you both for listening to detail after detail during walks and for always saying yes, and with such enthusiasm, when I ask if you'll read yet another version of yet another piece of writing.

A special thank you to my children—Kathleen, Bobby, Jack, and Sam—who have been not only supportive but who have also provided many not-always-intentional distractions. Thank you for keeping the humor in all these years of writing. Thanks also to Sam L., Claire, Taylor, and Katherine for magnifying the fun and support, and to Mack, Lily, Wynn, Ro, Ruby, and Mclin for thinking my study is as magical as I do.

Finally, my deepest gratitude to Cal for all the years of love and support and for working with me so our marriage could expand to encompass my enormous need for time to myself. Thank you especially for minding the fort when the kids were little so I could leave for weeks at a time to attend writing workshops. Thank you for loving the same books I do, for being interested and interesting, and in recent years, thank you for all the dinners. Thank you, thank you for liking Provincetown. And most especially, thank you for never once suggesting I do something else. Cheers to what comes next.

Reading Group Guide for
Tidal Flats

This is the story of a marriage.

A young couple must navigate the fine line between the things they want for themselves and the life they want together, and it appears that each will have to make the same choice—the person they love or the life they want.

QUESTIONS & TOPICS FOR DISCUSSION

1. Husbands and wives make agreements—small, unspoken ones and larger ones that can be deal-breakers. What do you think of the agreement that Cass and Ethan made before they got married? Was there another way for them to work out their differences and still stay together? Do you think of marriage vows as an agreement?

2. At the halfway point in the book, what have Cass and Ethan learned about each other and about marriage?

3. The senior living arrangement at Howell is based on that of a family. Do you think it's a viable alternative to group homes?

4. The Fates acquired the nickname "Fates" long before Cass arrived at Howell House. How do you think that came about? What do you think Cass meant when she said she took their nickname as a sign?

5. In the novel, we get glimpses of Afghanistan. Discuss the different ways we're able to see into that country. Did you learn anything surprising?

6. What do you think of Ethan's project to put cameras in the hands of the Afghans?

7. What are your thoughts about Setara? How do you think being an Afghan and living in Afghanistan made her who she is?

8. Families of origin are powerful influencers. How did Cass's and Ethan's families of origin affect their marriage?

9. Do you think Vee is a good friend? Do you agree with her advice to Cass?

10. What do you think of Singer? Is he good for Cass?

11. Discuss the book's title. How does it apply to Ethan and Cass's relationship? How does it apply to the other characters and their relationships?

12. A number of books are not only mentioned but are a part of the story. How do they add to the overall experience of reading *Tidal Flats*?

13. We see many different marriages in the novel. Discuss the ways in which each one works or doesn't work.

14. Are Cass and Ethan good for each other?

15. What do you think of Ethan's choices? Do you have confidence in him? How did you react when he came back from Afghanistan in Chapter 45?

16. In the end, what do you think Cass has decided? What would you have done?

17. The novel was partially inspired by Steve McCurry's famous photograph "Afghan Girl." Did that add to the story?

18. By the end of the novel, what have Cass and Ethan learned about marriage?

19. Why might Ethan be the only person in the whole world Cass could forgive? What role does forgiveness play in *Tidal Flats*?

20. Did *Tidal Flats* change your perception of marriage in any way?

About the Author

Cynthia Newberry Martin holds an MFA from Vermont College of Fine Arts. She has served as the Review Editor for *Contrary Magazine* and the Writing Life Editor for *Hunger Mountain*. Her website features the How We Spend Our Days series, over a decade of essays by writers on their lives. She grew up in Atlanta and now lives in Columbus, Georgia, with her husband, and in Provincetown, Massachusetts, in a little house by the water. Her second novel, *Love Like This*, will be published in 2023.

yellow pear 🍐 press

Yellow Pear Press, established in 2015, publishes inspiring, charming, clever, distinctive, playful, imaginative, beautifully designed lifestyle books, cookbooks, literary fiction, notecards, and journals with a certain *joie de vivre* in both content and style. Yellow Pear Press books have been honored by the Independent Publisher Book (IPPY) Awards, National Indie Excellence Awards, Independent Press Awards, and International Book Awards. Reviews of our titles have appeared in Kirkus Reviews, Foreword Reviews, Booklist, Midwest Book Review, San Francisco Chronicle, and New York Journal of Books, among others. Yellow Pear Press joined forces with Mango Publishing in 2020, with the vision to continue publishing clever and innovative books. The fact that they're both named after fruit is a total coincidence.

We love hearing from our readers, so please stay in touch with us and follow us at:

> Facebook: Mango Publishing
> Twitter: @MangoPublishing
> Instagram: @MangoPublishing
> LinkedIn: Mango Publishing
> Pinterest: Mango Publishing
> Newsletter: mangopublishinggroup.com/newsletter

CPSIA information can be obtained
at www.ICGtesting.com
Printed in the USA
LVHW112059020822
725031LV00003B/234

9 781642 509816